Where Beautiful Inks

Love is Pain

1

A Poetic Anthology

Edited by:
Brandy Lane

Fort Wayne, Indiana

© 2024 Love is Pain; A Poetic Anthology
Editor: Brandy Lane
Foreword: Stevie Flood

Contributing Authors:
Kimberly LaSusa, Pendraig the Poet, Janaya Stephens, Ismet Diab,
Courtney Whittamore, Angela Psalm, Todd Worrell, Billie Jama,
Sara Jama, Ghada Khalil, Maria Thérèse Williams, Reena Doss,
Kalpesh Desai, Michael J. Dennis, Miriam Otto, Vaughn Roste,
Kelsey Annin, Stevie Flood, Brandy Lane

Published in the United States of America by:
Where Beautiful Inks LLC
Fort Wayne, Indiana

ISBN: 978-1-7363268-7-9

Library of Congress Control Number: 2024905084

All pictures throughout this book are available through
Canva and Canva Pro.

DEDICATION

To all of those who have loved, and lost...
but continue to love the lost.

TABLE OF CONTENTS

Kimberly LaSusa

Also known as kcl, Kim has set her poetry to go along with micro poems as the titles. Her style is sans punctuation or capitalization.

Pendraig The Poet

Pendraig has a Dragon as his likeness and often uses line breaks to punctuate, known as Enjambment.

Janaya Stephens

*Also known as LG

Ismet Diab

Due to the nature of Ismet's poetry, she does not title her poems.

Angela Psalm *continued*

Todd Worrell

Reena Doss

Kalpesh Desai

Stevie Flood

Brandy Lane

Brandy Lane *continued*

Where Beautiful Inks

Love is Pain

A poetic anthology

FOREWORD

Welcome, dear reader, to a journey through the tumultuous terrain of the human heart. Within the pages of this anthology, "Love is Pain," we embark on a voyage guided by the courageous voices of poets from every corner of the globe. Together, they weave a tapestry of emotion, exploring the complex interplay between love and pain—the ecstasy of connection, the agony of separation, and the bittersweet symphony of longing and loss. Love, that most beguiling of emotions, holds within its embrace the power to uplift and to devastate, to heal and to wound. It is a paradox—a delicate balance between joy and sorrow, passion and despair. And yet, for all its complexities, love remains an enduring force, shaping our lives in ways both profound and ineffable. In this collection, curated with care and insight by the visionary Brandy Leigh Lane, you will encounter a kaleidoscope of experiences, each poem a glimpse into the depths of the human soul. Through their words, these poets invite us to bear witness to the raw, unfiltered essence of love—to confront the shadows that lurk within our hearts and to celebrate the light that illuminates our darkest hours. As you turn these pages, allow yourself to be swept away by the power of verse, to be moved by the beauty of language and the resonance of shared experience. For within these lines, you will find solace in the knowledge that you are not alone—that love, in all its pain and glory, unites us in our humanity. So, dear reader, open your heart and brace yourself for the journey ahead. For in the exploration of love's complexities, we discover not only the depths of our own emotions but also the profound beauty of the human spirit.

Stevie Flood

*Edited for grammatical errors. Some capitalizations and punctuation preferences are left for artistic effect at the request of the individual authors.

Also, slight variations in local word use and spellings appear, depending on where the poet resides. American English slightly varies from British English.

About the Author

Kimberly LaSusa (kcl)

Kimberly LaSusa, 52, lives in New York and is the mom of two humans and two cats that have taken solemn vows to never cuddle with people. (The cats, not the humans).
She works in finance by day, spending her free time in her garden and writing under the pen name "kcl".
A free verse poet with the need to capture moments of emotion, Kim hopes to keep sharing her words with others.

You can find her on Instagram (www.instagram.com/kcl_words) and Facebook (www.facebook.com/iamkclwords).

Kimberly has
a unique way
of portraying her
poetry.

She does not
title her poems,
nor does she
use any
punctuation
or capitalization.

In the place
of titles, there
are micro poem
companions that
blend well into
the longer poem.

Kimberly LaSusa

Kimberly LaSusa

for being soft has exhausted me
my insides being torn from my body
tossed to the wind where they twist
and bend at the world's whim
and i feel every living thing around me
every part of them like the forced air
of a storm pushing itself through me

it is so very easy to take me for granted
with my forgiveness and gentle hands
so very easy to ignore the bruises
that cover the inside of my skin
gifts from those who are trying to
navigate their own tornados or those
who wouldn't be bothered to stop to look
for them after hurling stones anyways

yet when i harden my skin into
a mirror of their behavior
they do not revel in the cuts that
their mimicked mouths make and
to be honest it's even more exhausting
to change my nature

so can i please just be done
for dealing with people
has used up all i have to give

-kcl

2

Love is Pain

*y*ou slowly
stripped me down
of everything you said
you loved about me
and then claimed
my insufficiencies
had killed us

dragging your
darted tongue
across the raw flesh
left behind
to taste your victory
then walking away
with pieces of
me dripping
from your
gluttoned skin

i leave me laid here
my bones taking
a moment to
breathe in the
stale copper air
before it's time to
rearrange themselves
into whomever i will be
now that you stole
who i was before

*i wonder who i
will be this time*

-kd

3

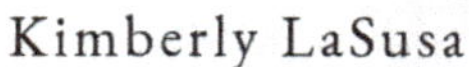
Kimberly LaSusa

did you mean to kill me
when you spoke that day?

you tried to
take them back
the words you so
neglectfully
flung at my feet
but it's far too late
for i have already
consumed them whole
they live in me now
etched on the
inside of my skin
decorating me in shadows
they are my epitaph
and i have become
my own graveyard

-kcl

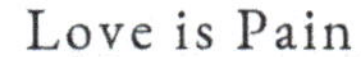

*h*ow easily
you burn
my flesh
without
a thought
and you
dare leave
flowers
for my
charred
bones
to hold?

with arms full of ash and
the brightest of Blugloss

Kimberly LaSusa

in the cold grey
space your hands left
a weeping grove of
cypress sprung

my asylum

♡-kcl

Love is Pain

i gather the feathers to
sleep on

i was love

but his haunted heart
has consumed
every part of me
and i am left empty

undead

a home for
mockingbirds.

-kcl

Kimberly LaSusa

of all the things
we carry,
the sorrow of regret
is the heaviest

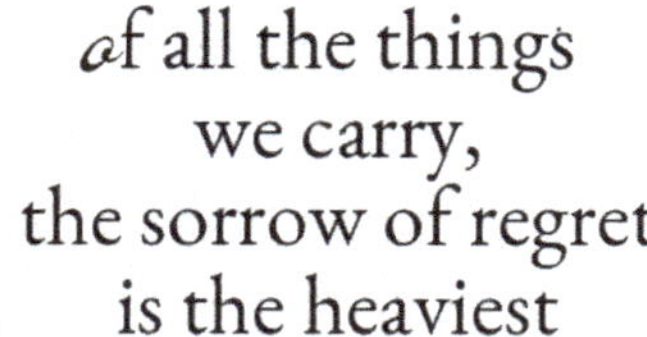

Love is Pain

i am helpless
in my regret
a dead tree

fallen

this stagnant
lake, a grave

the edges of
my wooden corpse
bloated into
soft splinters
and body steeped
with murky blood
i carved from
my mistakes

-kd

Kimberly LaSusa

he said he was sorry
and we pass each other
a hundred times a day
the cats have taken sides
but they haven't whispered
the secret to the little ones yet

i'm prone to sleepwalking now
as red paint drips from my ears
i use it as rouge so my children
can't see that i'm dead

they dance in it, unknowingly
jumping into shallow puddles
like after the storm

it covers everything

staining the floors
(their skin)
the glass in the windows
sitting in the frames
hanging on our walls
and colors our lips as we
sit for Sunday Dinner

but he doesn't seem
to mind the taste

-kcl

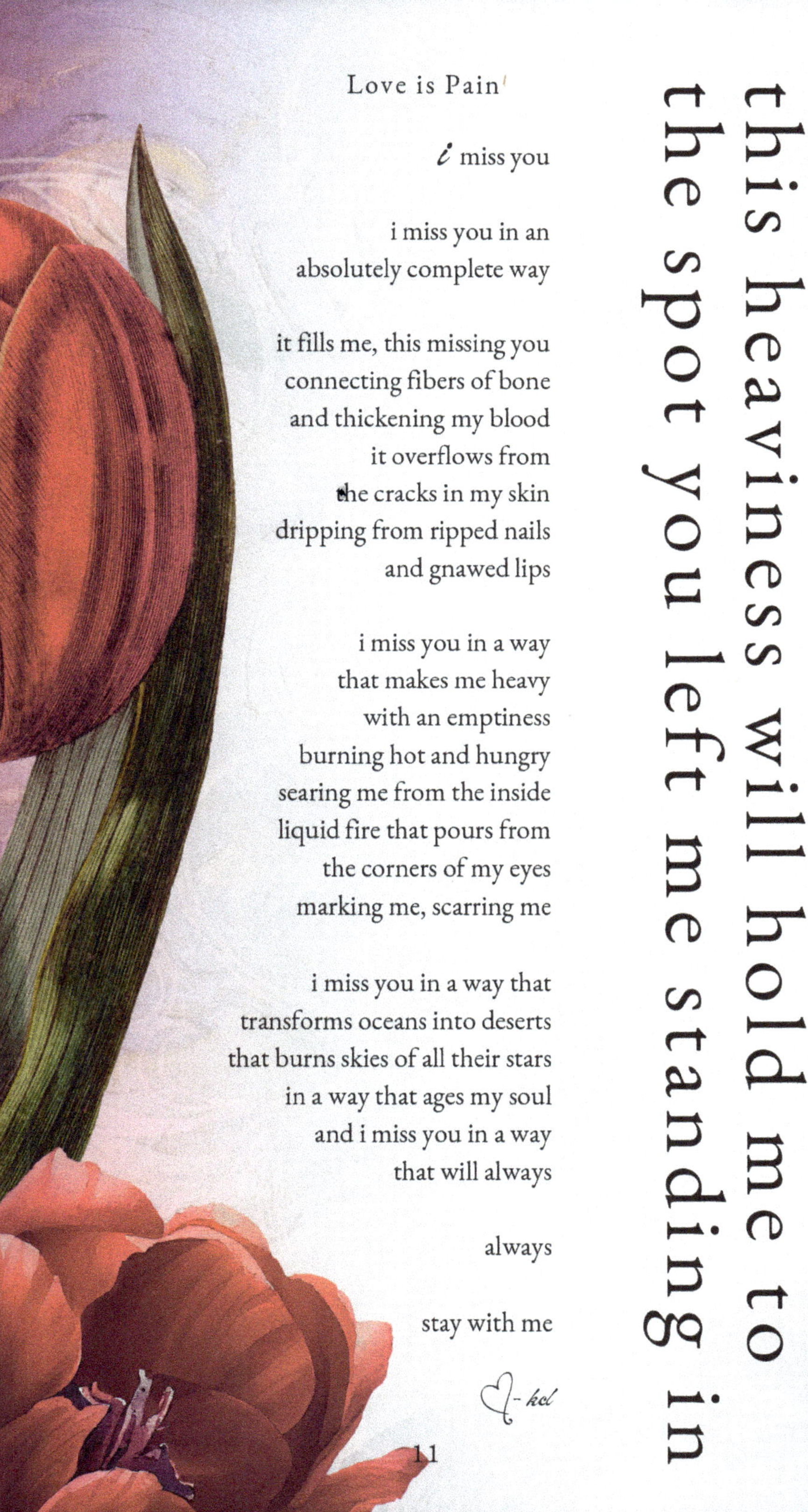

Love is Pain

i miss you

i miss you in an
absolutely complete way

it fills me, this missing you
connecting fibers of bone
and thickening my blood
it overflows from
the cracks in my skin
dripping from ripped nails
and gnawed lips

i miss you in a way
that makes me heavy
with an emptiness
burning hot and hungry
searing me from the inside
liquid fire that pours from
the corners of my eyes
marking me, scarring me

i miss you in a way that
transforms oceans into deserts
that burns skies of all their stars
in a way that ages my soul
and i miss you in a way
that will always

always

stay with me

— kcl

on the days it hurts the
worst, I remind myself that
sometimes rebirth can feel
a lot like dying

-kcl

*i*t rushes in looking to drown
as water, searching for the cracks
lined in sharpness
like words that bleed you;

for the hidden gaps that echo
through unseen vastness
hoping to slide into narrow slips of space
large enough to hold worlds,
to hold wounds of tutored fear;

cold disquietude hunting for gashes
filled with savage silence,
with doubts that tear back the edges
of your skin until you are raw;

i can feel it moving, deep inside
forming a rotted labyrinth
erosion trailed behind to birth new fissures
threatening to break me

to break me
break me

or make me

—kcl

Kimberly LaSusa

i always thought death
would be a silent thing

*y*ou left

the words
like sirens
in my ears

even the air
around me
became so loud
that i did not
hear my heart die

and my soul
did howl then
loudly again, so loudly
that the earth
shook in
gale wind

for there are
some pains
too great to be
suffered alone

in silence

-kcl

Love is Pain

*y*our name
stays with me

it's stuck to
the roof of
my mouth
where i spend
hours trying
to pry you
out with my
tongue

all the while
craving it's
bitter taste

my mouth
fills with
blood as
teeth catch
the edge
of my cheek
and i force
myself
to drink down
each sickly
sweet unspoken
thought of
missing you

♡ -kd

i have to let you go or
i'll never stop bleeding

Kimberly LaSusa

*t*he air cuts me
dressing my bruised
husk in deep lines
and i can't get
small enough to
catch my breath

small enough to
cocoon myself
away from sharp
careless blades of
selfish tongues and
hands and minds

i just want to hide
in some dark corner
some quiet corner
and collect all the
pieces of myself
that i have lost or
had stolen from me

to witness the
insincere world
from a distance

Love is Pain

i feel far too real
standing here in
my stained skin
dressed in evidence
of mislaid trust
clutching red jade

watching color
drip to the floor
as i pray for the
safety of smallness

-kcl

About the Author

Pendraig the Poet

Pendraig the poet is based in North Wales and writes on many different themes, including contemporary pieces about the human experience, societal, political and environmental issues. Pendraig has been published in numerous anthologies and is also the editor and publisher of Carnyx Collective anthology, which raises funds for charitable causes. Find more of Pendraig's work here:

FB:- **https://www.facebook.com/profile.php?id=100083281543819**

X:- http://twitter.com/@Pendraigthepoet

Lovely Lines

My Friend

Red

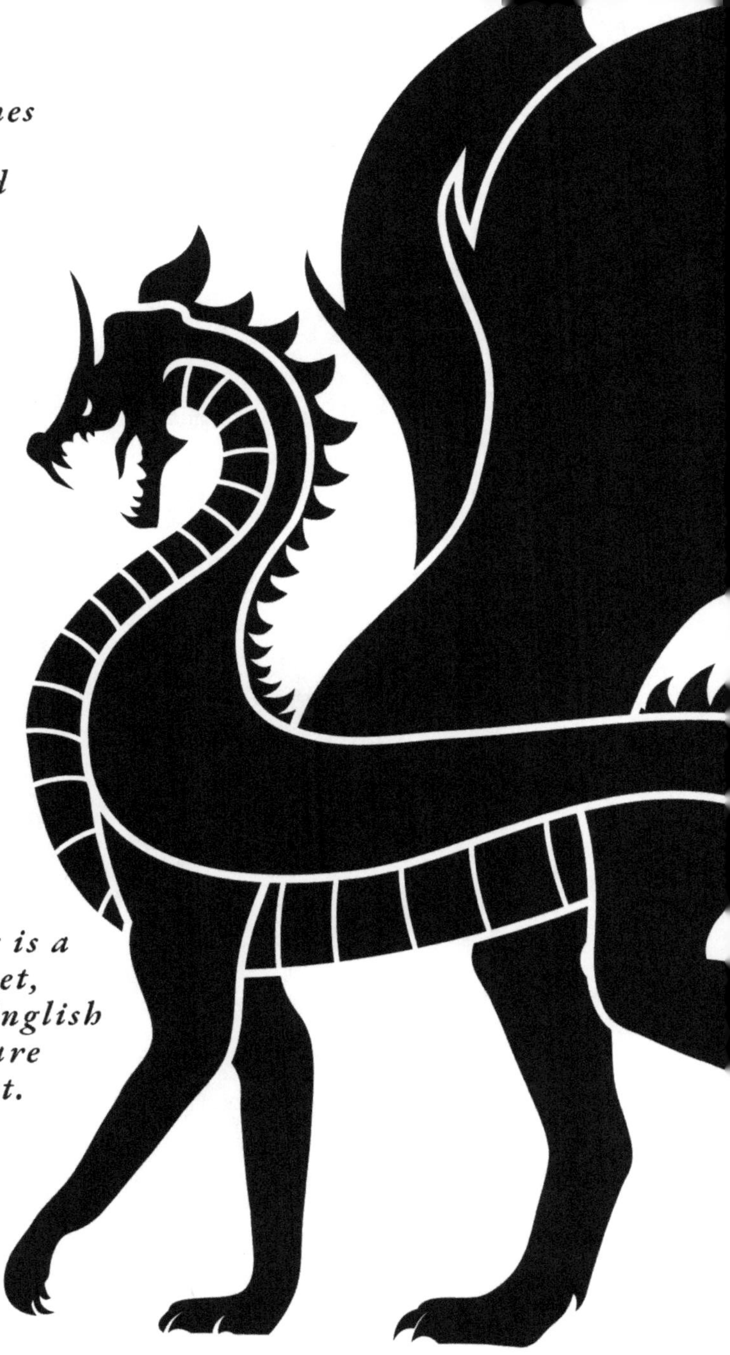

Pendraig the Poet

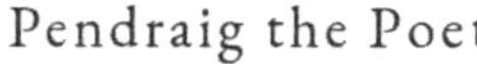

Pendraig the Poet

Saw her the other day
Just from a safe distance
Up close in personal space
There would be no resistance
She would have her way

Her beautiful lines were read
And all that she suggested
With words of such loveliness
In the mind's eye digested
Everything that her body said

So analogous of one another
Although she had no parallel
Her curvature sure to allure
Under heels a head fell
Then heart had to recover

When as if recognising reflections
Each pair of eyes met
An act of interlocking individuals
Paths pre-determined and set
Walking away in different directions

Pendraig

Lovely Lines

My Friend

Mon Amie
  Come sit with me
  To tell tales of old
  Upon a bench
  Under a tree
  Let's reminisce
  When we too
  Were free
  Before becoming cold

    My dear friend
      In the end
      If I be so bold
      Upon my honour
      Under a spell
      We do exist
      For you and I
      We live a lie
      If the truth be told

        My bosom buddy
          With waters muddy
        Overgrown with mould
          Upon humans being
          Under the thumb
          Though we resist
          We don't see
          What could be
        Just what we are sold

      Pendraig

Red

He was wolf
Wearing wool
She was red
To a bull
Ready to ride
Lost in thought
Her scent
He caught
Upon the air
Alluring him
Enchanting, enticing
Beckoning

Into the wood
To her lair
Looking good
Enough to eat
She uncloaked
Her form
Sickly sweet
Smooth and soft
Like lamb's skin
She loosed
Her hair
While speaking

Flirtatious, forlorn
Teasing his tail
Lust was born
Under her hood
He devoured her
She tasted good
Innate instinct
They howled
In sync
With delight
Riding, without pause
Throughout the night

Love is Pain

Abiding, without bite
Yet wolfish grin
Within her den
Beneath blue moon
Lingering longing
Long before
Legend and lore
Cautionary tales
Those twisted
Truths of yore
She was red
She was wolf

When granny told
Her betrothed
Did discover
She had lain
With another
With axe aloof
Wolf was slain
She returned
In sheep's clothing
To the flock
With sheepish grin
Her basket full

Pendraig

About the Author

Janaya Stephens (LG)

Janaya Stephens joined Instagram under the handle @throughthelookingglasspoet, which was quickly and endearingly shortened to "LG"—which has become her pen name. She has always loved poetry and began writing at a very young age. In university, she played for the varsity basketball team; sports have always been her passion. Her majors were English literature and drama. While at university, she was cast in the stage production of Romeo and Juliet and found her true calling. She then went to theatre school in Toronto and has since begun a successful career in film and television. Janaya is a Canadian mother. She has a daughter and a son. When COVID hit, she was inspired to start writing again and discovered the poetry community on Instagram. It was there that she found enjoyment in reading others' poetry. Her live shows are popular, and her love of entertaining shines through.

Janaya's most poignant pieces seem to stem from her experiences as a mother and her love for them. Nostalgia and time are recurring themes, as is a good dose of self-reflection. Janaya has just released her first book of poetry, A Little Red Book of Poetry, which is available on Amazon: https://mybook.to/Littleredbook

She is also working on a book of prose and short stories based on the true story of her experiences with her daughter when she was very ill and the ongoing challenges that they still face. Janaya has written a screenplay on the subject matter and a one-woman show for the stage. It just seems natural now to write a book.

Janaya Stephens

Janaya Stephens

In the eye of a storm,
a flurry of dagger words
whips 'round and cuts right through—
piercing the inner ear,
bleeding out all other sounds.
Just a vacuum of rage
from which you tried
to not engage.

You saw it coming,
you always do.
It is not the first time,
and no matter what you do
(or don't do)
it follows you.

Your senses peaked,
 trembling—but in a guard stance.

On thin ice, you tread
with every syllable you speak,
every breath, even the meek—
yet still, at the same time,
trying not to be weak.

Love is Pain

How is this my life? You wonder.
But how could it not be?
How could I afford to...

This is my home and
this is now me—
available and hanging like fresh meat
because this is where the children and I sleep.

Like a punching bag,
receiving all their troubles,
blow after blow,
time and again.

Janaya Stephens

The children will hear, surely...
that is *your* number one concern.

But, this enrages your enemy—
your focus on him he demands,
and you ready your hands to block—
in case he clocks
 your escape, and any plans
you might think to make.

He resides under lawful radar.
 No black eyes. No evidence.

But there once was the smell of pickles.

The jar he chased after you with
as you attempted to ascend
the stairs away from him.
It's what was on hand.
He caught you from behind
and proceeded to dump
that jar of pickles over you.

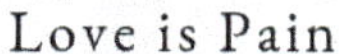

A jar of fucking pickles.

Mom,
I want to thank you,
I have always loved pickles.
I was allowed to.
And, like everything else you have done,
you protected us
and our chance to fall in love...
with pickles.

But, I'm not sure I will ever *not* think
of what a jar of pickles can mean.
I will still love them
because, for me
they represent
your strength to leave.

Tiny Shoes

Today, it was the tiny shoes.
And the way they never fit you.
Scattered across the floor.
Some, without pairs.
Adorable tiny little shoes.
They were everywhere.

I washed the tiny spoons.
Little pieces of orange,
I threw in the bin.
Wiped clean, the high hair.
Mopped "feeding time" from the floor.
Remembering
all this—
and so much more.

This is a place I've been.

But this is not *my* place—
the actual space.

I am just the maid.
Living memories
in retrograde.
Swells fill my eyes.
I choke down waves;
heavy pressure lies.

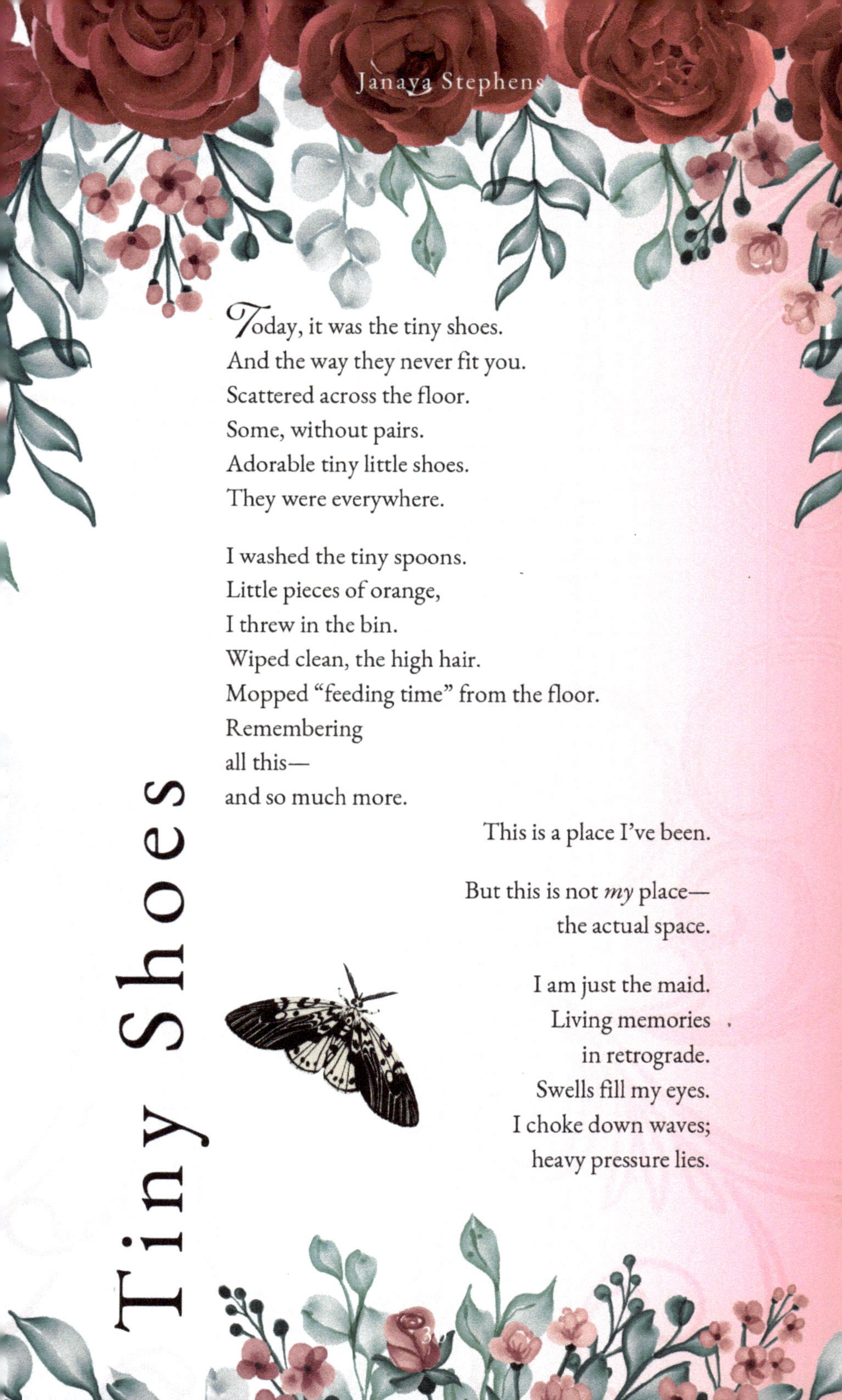

What is this nostalgic beast
that grows with teeth,
chewing my insides?

It's the threat of death
that came for you
when you should have been wearing
tiny shoes.

Your feet are as big as mine now;
this is everything that counts.

So why does the sight
of so many tiny shoes
make me want to cry?

They were everywhere.

So before I went home,
I arranged them with care.

Each one weighted, like a stone.

♡ -LG

Janaya Stephens

I see the box.
I've been here since it was built.

Yes,
I know what the label says:
it's not untrue.

But, do you see here?
This is a big box,
not even 20% filled.
There are so many more spaces
on its outer layer
for more labels;
if that's what you want to call them—
if we must use that word.

And see here, my love,
the stickers are blank,
and you can write
whatever you want
in the space.

Love is Pain

Maybe someday
you'll brave your way
out of the box.
The box does not define you,
but it did keep you safe
and will always be there.
It's a safe space.

But, my beautiful girl,
safe is not a place to stay!
Safe can be a cage;
there is no room for growth;
there is no escape.

So keep the box,
but be brave.

Nothing stays the same.

♡LG

Janaya Stephens

The Daughter

Her pleas:
I don't want to grow up.
I'm scared of the future.
I don't want to live alone.
I'll always play with my toys.
The floor, scattered with them all...
Frantic.
She's clinging and searching
for joy.
Today's outfit, planned.
Clothes that are too small—
she refuses to be tall.

The Mother

Her side:
I don't want to grow old.
I'm worried about the future.
I don't want to live alone.
I'll always have brown hair.
Coloured dye staining
the counter, her fingers.
Resistance.
She's clinging to
her youth today
covering grey strays—
she refuses to fade.

Mother and Daughter, Both

In hormonal storms;
raging within.
On the verge of big changes
that feel like cliffs.

They hold each other,
because neither of them
feel like letting go.

♡-LG

Janaya Stephens

A burden:

"It's something painful you must carry,
even though it hurts you very much."

It's something that you tuck away
deep down inside
as far as you can
so that you can make room
for all the other things,
but it never really goes away.

A burden is something you carry
while trying to build the blocks of joy
while trying to remain present
in the moment that is here today.

But that burden sneaks up
on a grey day;
it will always replay,
it is here to stay.

The Burden

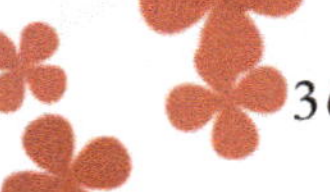

Love is Pain

You carry the weight
of mistakes you've made;
days that didn't go your way

There is strength required
to carry them.

Every one of them like patchwork,
in the fabric of your story.

And I'm here for yours, lover;
I'm here to help you
distribute the weight.
If we carry them together,
it won't be so great.

Janaya Stephens

Wings and Cages

$\mathcal{I}$ beat
back the
wings that poke
from my flesh—
the soul that would
break free.
But the heart now knows;
it is the wings
that have but only
caged me.

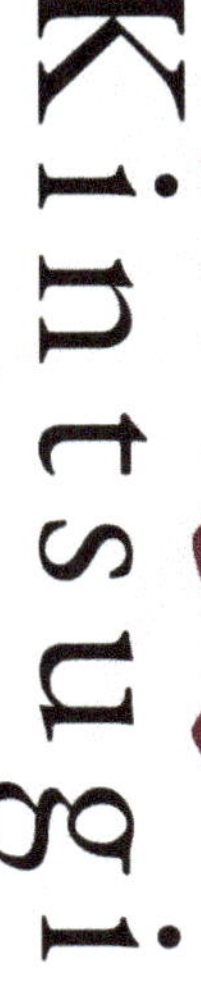

Kintsugi

And this heart,
albeit cracked;
this soul,
albeit weathered,
will not shatter,
but rather
will be gilded
with a golden tireless spirit—
will be forged stronger.

The breakage celebrated—
showcasing a journey,
a history,
a memorial of battle scars—
tissue and sinew reinforced,
and therefore
better equipped
for future storms.

♡-LG

Janaya Stephens

I Dare Not

There are secrets in my heart
that I dare not even tell myself.
I can feel their shadows.
I can feel they're dark.
I dare not,
or the whole of me may collapse,
folded into the void.

I beat them back
when they start trying to speak.
I beat them back—
muzzled their sound,
for I could never let them speak.
I muzzled their sound
so as not to drown
I could never let them speak freely.

Some things
belong in the vault.
Some things are likely,
and
some things are not
my fault.

Those from the crypt,
from a life lived.

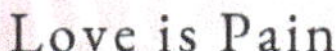

Love is Pain

Things that never left—
just buried in the depths
of my soul.

The weight—so great,
it takes all of my strength.
The pressure
makes it hard to breathe.

And I need to keep breathing.
I have little people
depending on me.
Time travel to go back
to change
is not possible.

Don't try to save me.
I got this.

I swallow the sounds
down.
Forcibly.
They will never have their day.

Because this,
well, this
is a new day
to my grave.

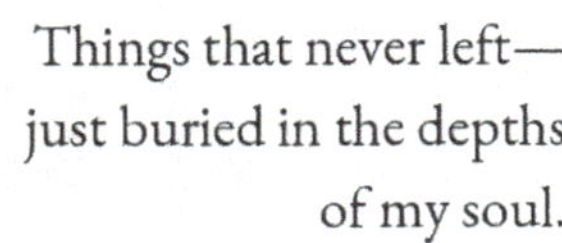

Janaya Stephens

The Bird

The words that I spill
rush forth for the kill;
the passion inside
will never be still.
This page must be filled
from bone deep to the quill;
out they pour,
breaching the brim.

My soul, all twisted,
I spit and I scream;
I rage hard when I need,
I dream free when I breathe.

And as much as I try
to untie this knot from within,
it's what gets me by.

It's a reason why.
It's my place to begin.

It's a slip knot, but
seafarer strength;
tight with a bite
like the blade of a knife.

I fight with my grip,
but it burns the skin.
Friction, hot heat—
so I continue to bleed.

The depth of the red
keeps me warm and fed.
The drops at my feet
pool around like the sea.

Love is Pain

This is my room.

And what do we have here?
Out the window, there is
a bird that looms;
it flies right for me.

To save me?
Implore me?
Berate me?
Adore me?

Knocked down by the glass
now dead in the grass.
You didn't see that, did you?
...stupid bird.

So you assumed
you'd swoop in and save me?

Who's next I wonder—
to reach for the save?
Only to find
this isn't a game.

I am not lame.
I am a flame.
There is nothing you have
from which I can gain.

There is no way in,
but if you must,
you can watch
because there is no way out.

I carry my own cross.

The struggle is fine;
it's been here for a time,
and you aren't the first
to wanna call me your "mine."

If I had a dime...

♡-LG

Janaya Stephens

*N*estled behind the smile
Is a raging bull on idle.
Rusted are the blades
used many a time to save.

Beware the jaws that bite,
for there are claws that catch.

What see you in me?
A happy little bee?
A receiver on bent knee?
Sponge-like, filled with glee?

I could tell you the tales
of cross-stitch patterns
mixed with a twist of
darkened fabrics'
cotton-candy sweetness,
warm woolen comfort,
and silk-satin lying.
Through your feed, I'm hiding.

And maybe you believe me.
Maybe it's not a lie.
Perhaps the battle rages.
It comes and goes in stages.

Longtime, my inner foe, I sought
and drank it dead with eyes aflame.
Straight like a shot, without blame.

The Blade

Love is Pain

For these demons,
they were only mine,
chewing on decaying rinds.

With my soul, they were bought.
And the regret...
It stinks like rot.

Yet, are they slain?

And what of the beast,
Presumably deceased?
What evidence have you got,
for there is no recognizable trace
of that contorted face?

In the attic closet,
with all the other things,
you will find the blade
used for the save.
Blood soaked—a rusted red,
from the moment it swung hard
and severed off the head,
which when plucked from the ground,
was tucked underarm.

She then grew her wings,
feathered, flying, and free.

Alice...
She now sings of other things.

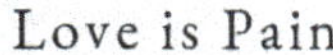

Janaya Stephens

Heavy

Heavy is the wait.
A two-year ton stone.
Heavy is the *weight*.

And I'm awake—
not to claim I'm *woke*—
for something inside
has definitely broke.

Trying to make amends
with the lost time.
Trying to calculate
what might have been gained;
counting up what remains,
calculating the cost.

Subtracting.

Subtracting.

Dividing.

Then multiplying.

Heavy

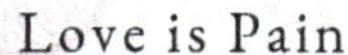

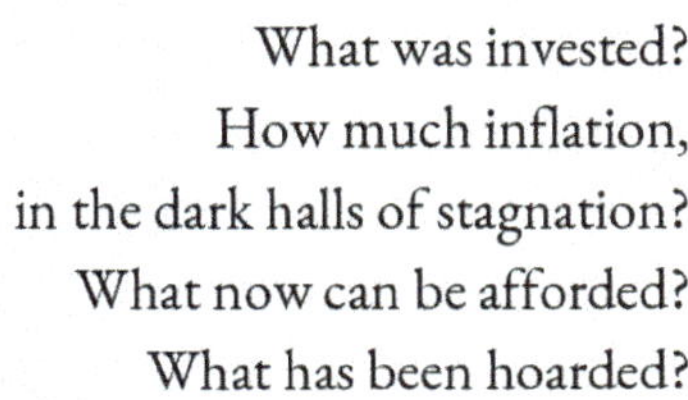

What was invested?
How much inflation,
in the dark halls of stagnation?
What now can be afforded?
What has been hoarded?

Changes and stalemates.
Broken down relations.

Need a vacation,
but not to relax.
I need a vacation *from* relaxing.
I need to hit the ground running—
crack the ground with each bound.
Make tracks,
and not look back.

I'm awake.
Repeat after me,
"There is no more waiting."

About the Author

Ismet Diab

Since October 2019, Ismet Diab (she/her), known on Instagram as @shespeaksyoursilence, has been transforming silence into expressive poetry. She chose this pen name because for her, silence was once a confining Pandora's box, but poetry became her key to freedom. Through her verses, Ismet releases pent-up emotions, untold stories, and hidden torments, giving a voice to the unspoken parts of her soul. Her poetry not only reflects her inner journey but also resonates with the experiences of others, as she empathetically navigates and narrates the untold tales of many.

Ismet's work delves into themes of love, grief, resilience, and the transformative journey from darkness to light, drawing readers into a world where each poem is a profound emotional journey. Based in Alexandria, Egypt, she continues to connect with a global audience.

Discover more of Ismet's poetic journey by exploring her debut poetry collection, *OCEANS 7*, available on Amazon worldwide. Join her vibrant community of followers and find your own freedom in her words.

Ismet has a distinct approach to poetry: she chooses not to title her poems. This decision allows the words to seamlessly flow from one poem to the next, creating a continuous stream of thought and emotion.

Additionally, she uses minimal punctuation, further enhancing this sense of unbroken narrative. This style invites readers to journey through her poems as one cohesive experience, where each piece effortlessly blends into the next, offering a unique and immersive reading adventure.

All 6 pieces are from her debut collection "Oceans 7" which is available on Amazon.

Ismet Diab

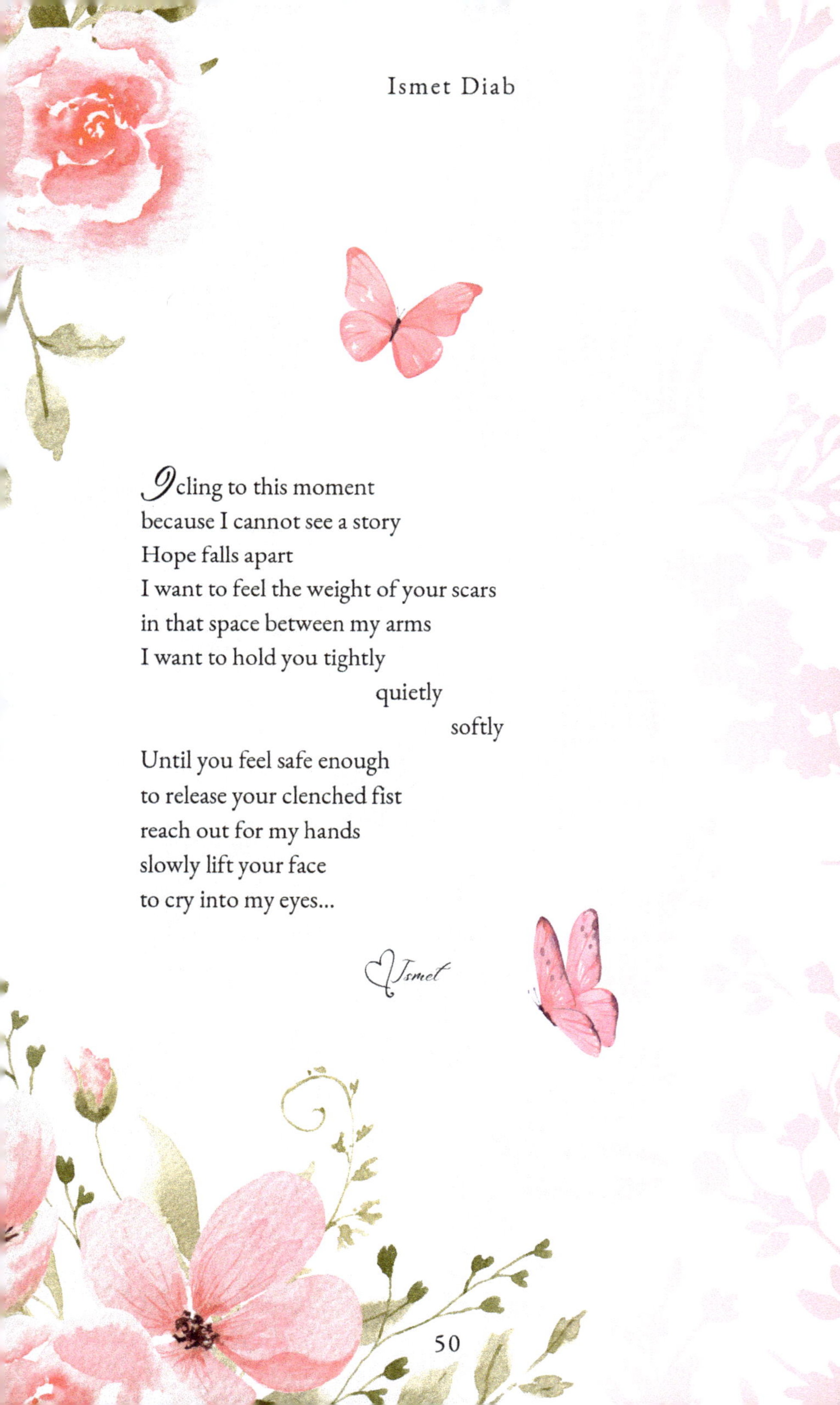

Ismet Diab

I cling to this moment
because I cannot see a story
Hope falls apart
I want to feel the weight of your scars
in that space between my arms
I want to hold you tightly

quietly

softly

Until you feel safe enough
to release your clenched fist
reach out for my hands
slowly lift your face
to cry into my eyes...

Ismet

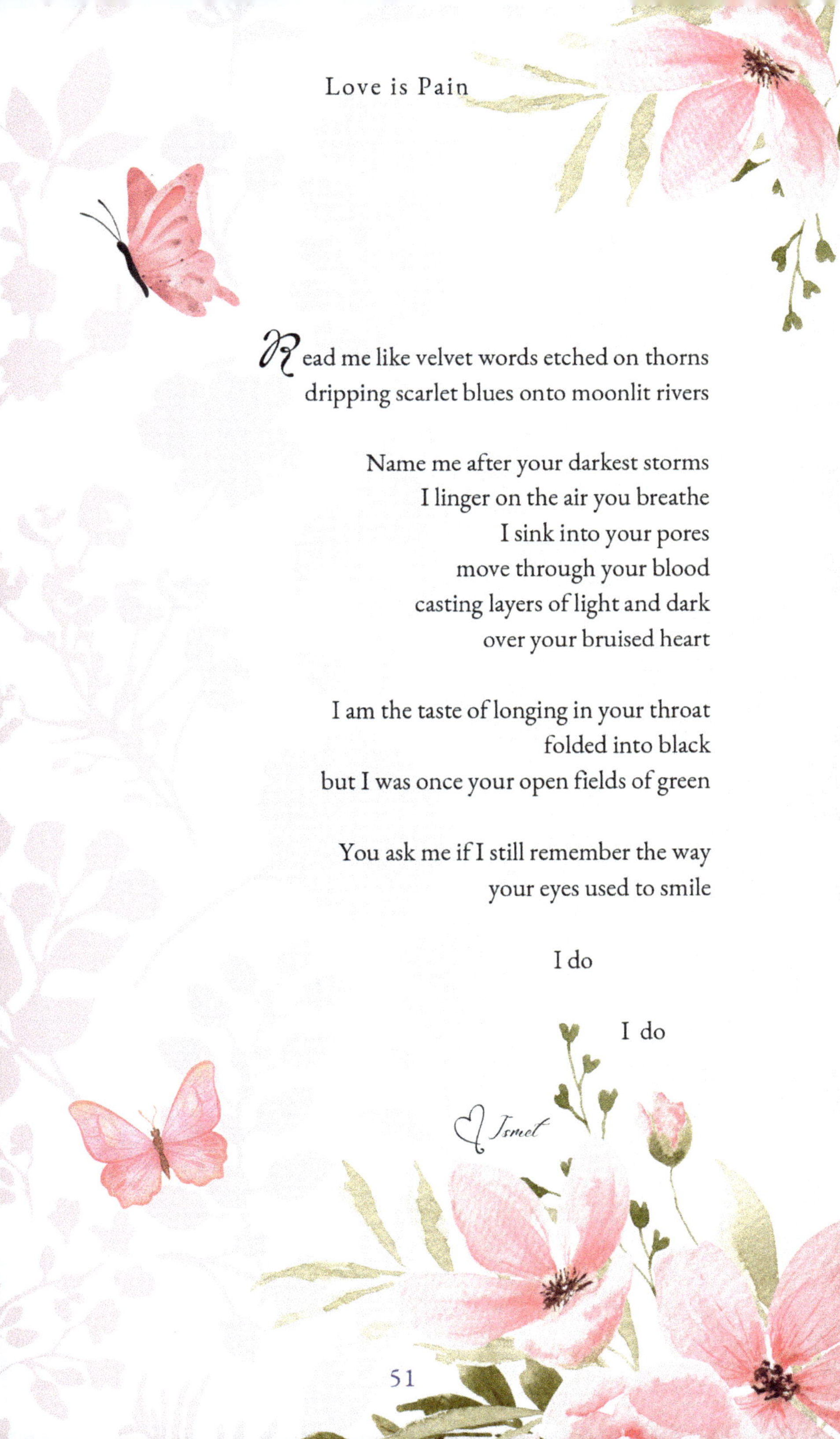

Love is Pain

Read me like velvet words etched on thorns
dripping scarlet blues onto moonlit rivers

Name me after your darkest storms
I linger on the air you breathe
I sink into your pores
move through your blood
casting layers of light and dark
over your bruised heart

I am the taste of longing in your throat
folded into black
but I was once your open fields of green

You ask me if I still remember the way
your eyes used to smile

I do

I do

Ismet

I lay on the rain-drenched grass
watching the birds fly

The trees dapple apricot-blue sunlight all over me
and if my pale skin glows in colors,
it is to surrender to the promise of the new day

There is a butterfly bandaging a ripped leaf
My fingers imitate its fluttering wings
as I tap my sternum ...

Yesterday's storm still lingers on my neck like a bruise

My heart bleeds poetry that leave my lungs,
leave my lips like white smoke that
gathers in the fleeting space between life and death
I choke on the words stuttering in my throat like a eulogy:

Everything beautiful reminds me of YOU

Ismet

Love is Pain

Pink pearled petals falling
Onto the sun kissed grass
Like butterfly wings
Waving goodbye
To the prettiest soul I have ever known

Thank you
For being the reason
To rekindle that light in my heart
That spark I believed was dimmed forever

The nostalgic perfume of the breeze
Moves into all my senses
Reminding me
There is a promise
In every spring

It always returns...

Ismet

I pour my heart in waves
onto my words
You feel the pulses of my veins
under your eyelids
Something in your heart
beats for me—
a forgotten feeling
a mystery

I am a gypsy
who knows how to dance
on quicksand
I make you dream
to tango with me
to the music of the falling rain
I spill my wildest dreams
into your blood
You feel the madness of my love
blowing embers in your heart
I am the thunder
slicing the stillness of your nights

You move through my poems
like a king
like a thief
like a wolf howling at the moon—
hungry for passion
thirsty for flames
In every version of you
you are a ghost
that keeps hunting me

I want to push you off
the margins of my pages
meet you in the depth of falling—
I float in the night sky...

waiting for sunrise

Ismet

*H*andful of ocean sands,
drenched in rain
It is holy the way earth crafts poetry
into honest hands:
that is to hold love like a bowl of fragile glass,
to be ready to bleed when it cracks,
to be brave enough to die inside
a thousand times
before we finally grasp life,
That is to pour out our pain like confessions,
That is to weave our brokenness
into a string of lights,
to save our hearts from darkness
I am haunted by the metaphors
I am haunted by how much I do not know of you
I am haunted by all this love
overflowing from my heart
I am longing to reach you
I am yearning to hold you
You see me silently
but you don't lower your defenses
and I... I am tired of

waiting

Ismet

About the Author

Courtney Whittamore

Courtney Whittamore is a person. She has done a lot of really fancy and interesting things in her life. One time, she convinced her younger siblings she was a vampire for a full week. Her brother lived in terror until her sister pointed out Courtney had a reflection. Thus, the ruse was shattered, but the magic was not. And so, she continues to sprinkle the world with wonder, light, laughter, and truth, wherever she goes.

She could tell you how she gets her theatrical flare for storytelling from her hilarious mother. And that she took that pizzazz and turned it into a career as a professional Broadway performer after attending the University of Cincinnati's College-Conservatory of Music for Musical Theatre. She could tell you about how success came and health went, leaving her with the task of changing dreams in her twenties. She could tell you that writing was her solace. She could tell you that the art of what she calls "word letting" saved her life.

But she would rather tell you again that she is a person. A person who writes. Mostly about humanity. And how humans are actually human, not societal machines made to live one way and one way only. She writes about what she has done. What has been done to her. About men who asked her to keep the door of possibility open when she shouldn't have. About bodies that don't want to exist under the conditions they are asked to operate under. About how being an adult is necessary but also a trap. And she writes about everything that never happened. Or did it?

You can find her writings over on her Instagram @courtney.whittamore where she posts the things she writes about being a person. Stay tuned, because she is always growing, always changing, and always encouraging you to be a person, too. She is working on her debut collection and many other surprise projects, so be sure to keep an eye out!

IG: @courtney.whittamore

He Loved the Idea

I Dare You

Tell Me Where It Hurts

Where Love Once Lived

Shower of Stars

I Won't Say I Love You

When Love Hit

It Starts With A Kiss

I Don't Want to be
Her Anymore

"T" for Trauma

The Rule of Staying

I Was Made for You

Courtney Whittamore

Courtney Whittamore

He Loved
the Idea

Sometimes I think
while tucked between sheets
that do not keep me warm,

"Who did he kiss goodnight?"

I want to believe it was me,
but hindsight disagrees,
and still repeats, incessantly,
he loved the idea,
he loved the idea,
of the bride inside his mind.

When he opened his eyes
to a blazing fire,
carefully, beautifully,
ignited beside him,
he only felt the burn
of everything
he didn't deserve.

I Dare You

I dare you.
Remind me why
this desperate fixation
to claim your mouth with mine
is worth my time.

I'll ignore your wants
until you know my dreams.
Yet I burn to
please you, tease you,
tumble in silken sheets with you.

I'm not the same
as what's her name,
so tell me why
our desire conspires with
constellations, crossed.

Gods softly sighing, smiling, their
divinity transpiring.
Tell me you believe in fate,
in sudden soulmates.

Tell me this isn't fake.
I dare you.

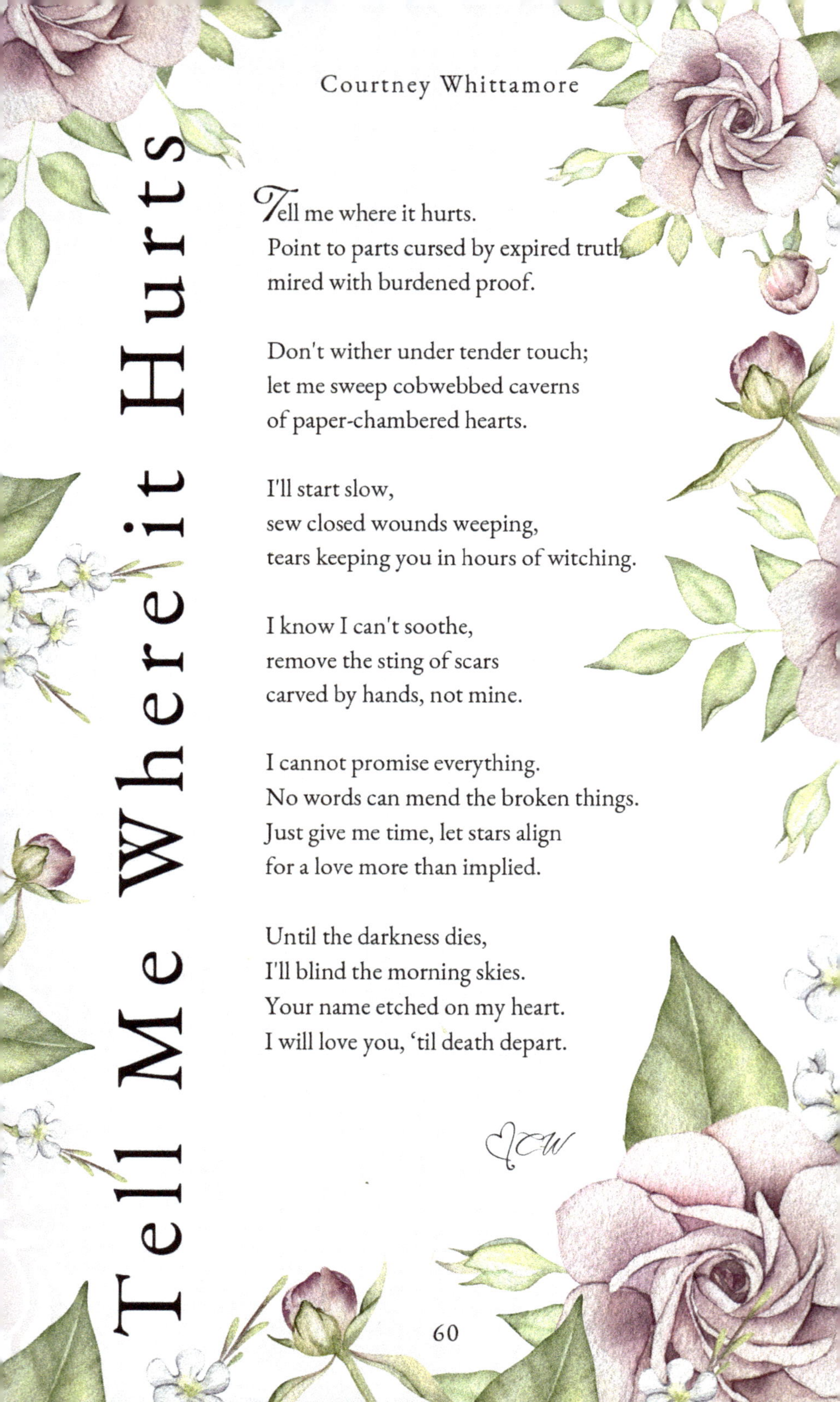

Courtney Whittamore

Tell me where it hurts.
Point to parts cursed by expired truth
mired with burdened proof.

Don't wither under tender touch;
let me sweep cobwebbed caverns
of paper-chambered hearts.

I'll start slow,
sew closed wounds weeping,
tears keeping you in hours of witching.

I know I can't soothe,
remove the sting of scars
carved by hands, not mine.

I cannot promise everything.
No words can mend the broken things.
Just give me time, let stars align
for a love more than implied.

Until the darkness dies,
I'll blind the morning skies.
Your name etched on my heart.
I will love you, 'til death depart.

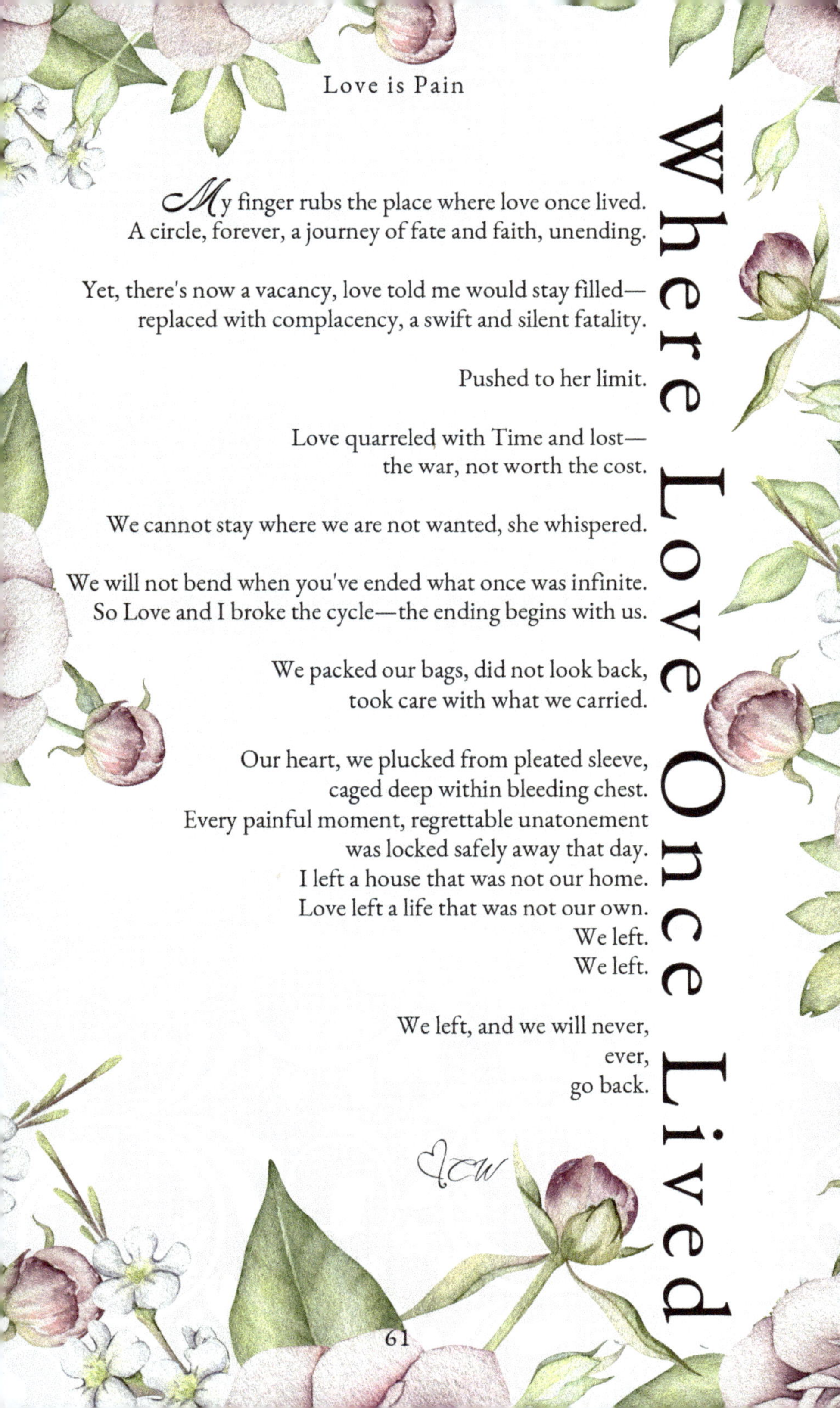

Love is Pain

My finger rubs the place where love once lived.
A circle, forever, a journey of fate and faith, unending.

Yet, there's now a vacancy, love told me would stay filled—
replaced with complacency, a swift and silent fatality.

Pushed to her limit.

Love quarreled with Time and lost—
the war, not worth the cost.

We cannot stay where we are not wanted, she whispered.

We will not bend when you've ended what once was infinite.
So Love and I broke the cycle—the ending begins with us.

We packed our bags, did not look back,
took care with what we carried.

Our heart, we plucked from pleated sleeve,
caged deep within bleeding chest.
Every painful moment, regrettable unatonement
was locked safely away that day.
I left a house that was not our home.
Love left a life that was not our own.
We left.
We left.

We left, and we will never,
ever,
go back.

Courtney Whittamore

Shower of Stars

I've never been one to twinkle.
I twine, ever thine, on vines
made of words and galaxies
only another universe can understand.

I am the tingling in your fingers
as you wake to take another day.
I wind through your mind
the moment you lose focus
because your heart
no longer adheres to normal time.

I add your skipped beats
to sheets of music to compose a score
only heard in your head
while it echoes in the heavens
alongside choirs I conduct in eternity.

I am the rhyme you sing under your breath
that always makes you smile,
this secret salacious libretto
always slipping where your sun won't shine.

Love is Pain

I am unearthly bright, white-hot delight
that excites and equally frights
in a sky, you cannot see.
I ignite sparks of dynamite
that blaze into fireworks or simply fire
depending on the night.

I am the shower of stars after, the embers
floating, coating your delicate awareness of
what is there and what is not.

I want to be known, I want to show you the
beauty in even the fallen stars.

But I've never been one to twinkle.
For I am the wrinkle in your timeline,
no one's understudy or byline,
I am the shining of dying suns
I am the thread of life, respun.

I'm am the whisper of bending trees
hoping one day,
maybe you can stand to actually believe
in that simple and silent wish
that will finally set me free
and we can love,
ensconced and entwined,
within infinity.

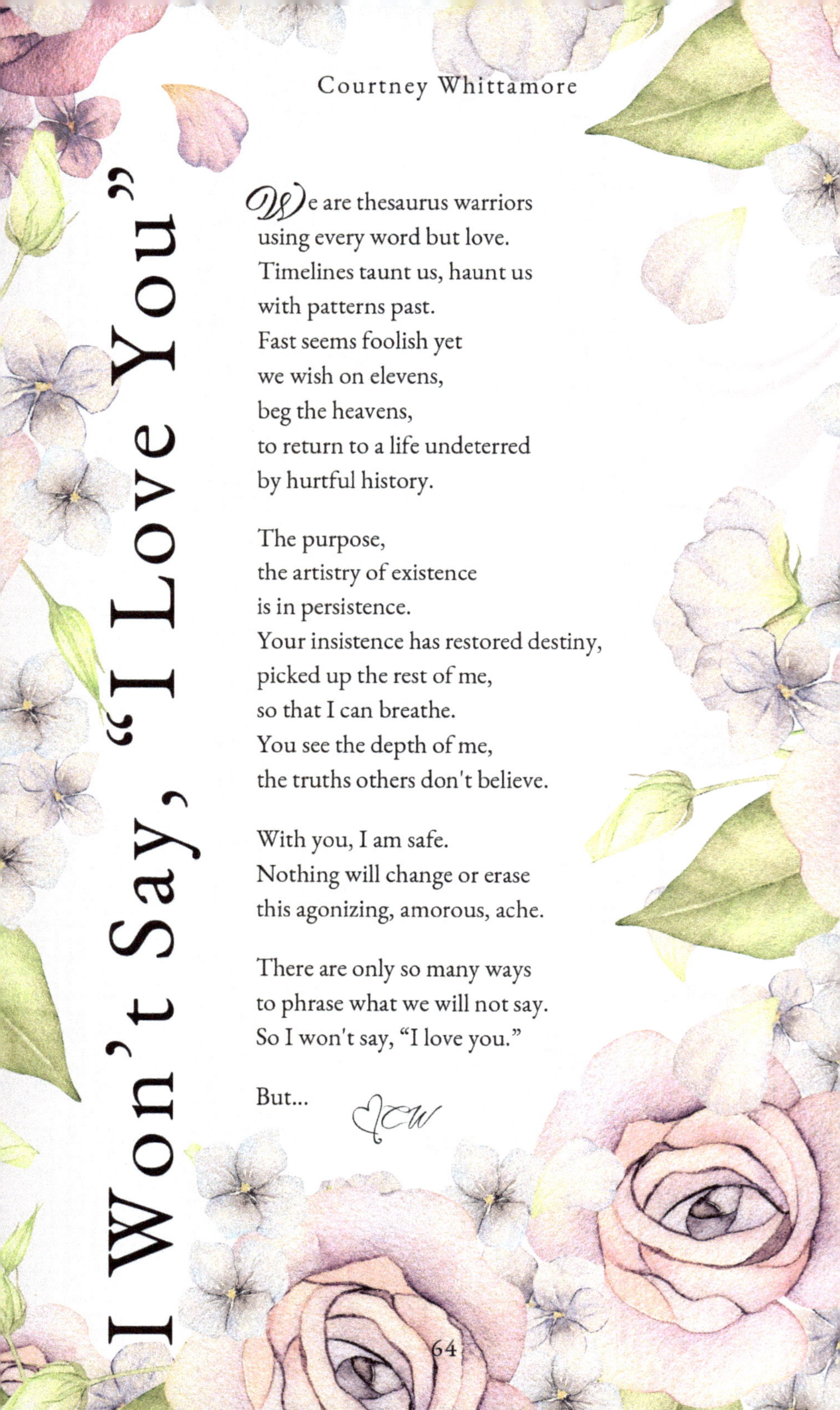

Courtney Whittamore

We are thesaurus warriors
using every word but love.
Timelines taunt us, haunt us
with patterns past.
Fast seems foolish yet
we wish on elevens,
beg the heavens,
to return to a life undeterred
by hurtful history.

The purpose,
the artistry of existence
is in persistence.
Your insistence has restored destiny,
picked up the rest of me,
so that I can breathe.
You see the depth of me,
the truths others don't believe.

With you, I am safe.
Nothing will change or erase
this agonizing, amorous, ache.

There are only so many ways
to phrase what we will not say.
So I won't say, "I love you."

But...

I Won't Say, "I Love You"

When Love Hit

When love hit me,
it fit between my ribs.
No skips, just slip
between skin that forgives.
I'll kiss away your sorrow,
borrow bones from tomorrow.
When love hit me,
I quickly gave way
Please, stay, remain
until our heart's decay.

Courtney Whittamore

Courtney Whittamore

A scene, only me, blown up on a movie screen.
Real life, but not quite, a plot I fought for despite not
knowing, just going, need guiding this fateful write.
Silver-and-white muddled twilight filters my winter
just right with glitter and shimmer. You just might
catch my bright side through my aged, hazy lens.

My heart thumps like a flash-pop—nerves jumbled as
heated glass drops, click-clack-clattering as it shatters
on the driver's side floor. My blood-red lips drip, drip,
slick with desire against the black-and-white set
design. Lick, haphazardly, look spectacularly, sharpen
vernacular, and wit fast as a whip.

I quickly quip a platitude, rehearsed absurdly,
"Hi, how are you?" before the action shot. Tilt here,
smile there, blissfully prepare as traffic horns blare,
and I snap back, an actress aware. This is no fairytale.
Heightened feelings everywhere—there's a plane on
the way containing a man I desperately believe lives a
life outside the one penned by my hand. Yes, it has the
shine of entertainment; this act of persuasion is
possibly insane, but the remaining refrain of reality
regains strength as I dramatically slam the breaks.

It Starts With A Kiss

Even under shadows of the bleakest kind. Inside my mind and otherwise, I find you—and I know of Technicolor hope. Colors crawl from corners, askew; you walk with vigor, power renewed. You flew here on the winds of change to claim a queen you didn't make. Symphony crescendo, lights turn up, so the increase in tempo matches rainbow-covered hello. I know just where to go around the back and to the side. I slide my arms around you.

No one else in view. No one else but you. And I know radical romance. Lips touch, brush as they advance this chance; only once isn't happenstance. I sigh, I rise, go slow, moan, so enchantment incants suspended dance, released. Your gentle hands sprout fingertip roots to plant on hips, slanted. Taking nothing for granted, you move, I approve. My tongue, your cheek, we seek to complete. Thoughts of scenes, screens, all manner of things fade and give way, like falling tides. One kiss, and I am felled under your spell.

I know true love.
And it starts with a kiss.
I know true love.
And it goes like this:

JCW

I Don't Want To Be Her Anymore

Courtney Whittamore

I don't want to be *her* anymore.
The *her* you held in your arms
like a lover, like a prisoner, like a prize,
like a trinket.

I don't want to be *her* anymore.
The *her* who waited at your door
for affection, for attention, for effort.

I don't want to be *her* anymore.
But I can't stop being *her* any more than I can
stop breathing, stop smiling, stop looking,
stop finding evergreen trees in a forest of decay,
silver linings when there's only rain,
rainbows and unicorns in a world of grey.

I don't want to be *her* anymore
because *she* loved you through rose-colored glasses,
and you didn't love *her*
through crystal clear eyesight—
and that bitch named Hindsight points out
every crack in the story I wrapped you in.

Like a prince among thieves.

Love is Pain

And, I don't want to be *her* anymore
because your love is no longer good here,
safe here, wanted here—but it's needed here—
it's the only proof of why I repeated every bad habit
I ever learned, when I was never taught how
to love right, sit tight, fight or flight, run tonight.

I don't want to be *her* anymore
because I don't have the papers that prove
she no longer belongs to you. I don't have
the ending to the story where *she* left,
but you were gone first.
I don't have the answers to why you
just ran out of love for *her*
when *she* filled you up with
all the love *she* had.

Where is the leak?
>Where is the crack?
>>Where is the reservoir that stores all *her* love
>>>because it surely didn't stay safely inside of you?

I don't want to be *her* anymore.
>**So, can you please sign the dotted line and set her free?**

Because I don't want to be *her* anymore, and you are the one who holds the pen that's always been mightier than the sword—that you drove through *her* spine the moment *she* left and didn't look back.

And as the door shut, you didn't see that you drove *her* to *her* knees, hands upturned to the sky that echoed, "Why?" Begging gods *she* didn't believe in to turn *her* into someone new—anyone would do so *she* didn't have to carry this...
This pain.
       This hurt.
              This love.
I don't want to be *her* anymore.
       I can't be *her* anymore.
She doesn't live here anymore.
       She doesn't exist here anymore.

I don't want to be *her* anymore
because *she* loves you,
and ***I can't love you anymore.***

Courtney Whittamore

"T" for Trauma

I close my eyes and sigh.
I tried counting the tiles lining the kitchen floor
to stop constantly keeping score.
In the war of myself against I,
none seem to see exactly where the sum of me ends,
and the none of me begins.
I am everything in this room—
and yet, I am nothing to you.

    If it were up to you, I'd be buried too—
       to hide the bruised, tender hues of
          black and blue tattoos blooming
             beneath my skin.

   And I don't know how I exhumed the smell of fumes
            left behind the night I set fire
              to paper-thin desire to stay,
      to find a way to save our ship from skimming
              tips of icebergs, unforgiving.

Love is Pain

I wither under the remembrance
the cold nights of December with frostbite
extending tenure into the next cycle of November
with only embers from fireside crackles—
crafted inside my drafty mind to keep me warm.

I close my eyes and sigh—lungs weighted with smoke and
whys. I despise myself for believing the lies
you fed me when we were fine.
I know this pyre to which I'm tied is only lit when I sink to
disparity's pit. And it's there I find you in this hellish dream—
this nowhere nightmare.

I close my eyes and sigh, but this time I smile— because
you're still there, tethered, ensnared, in no one's somewhere,
and you shiver, freeze, in a blustering breeze meant for me...
But you see, I'm released.

I open my eyes and sigh, and I finally feel relieved.

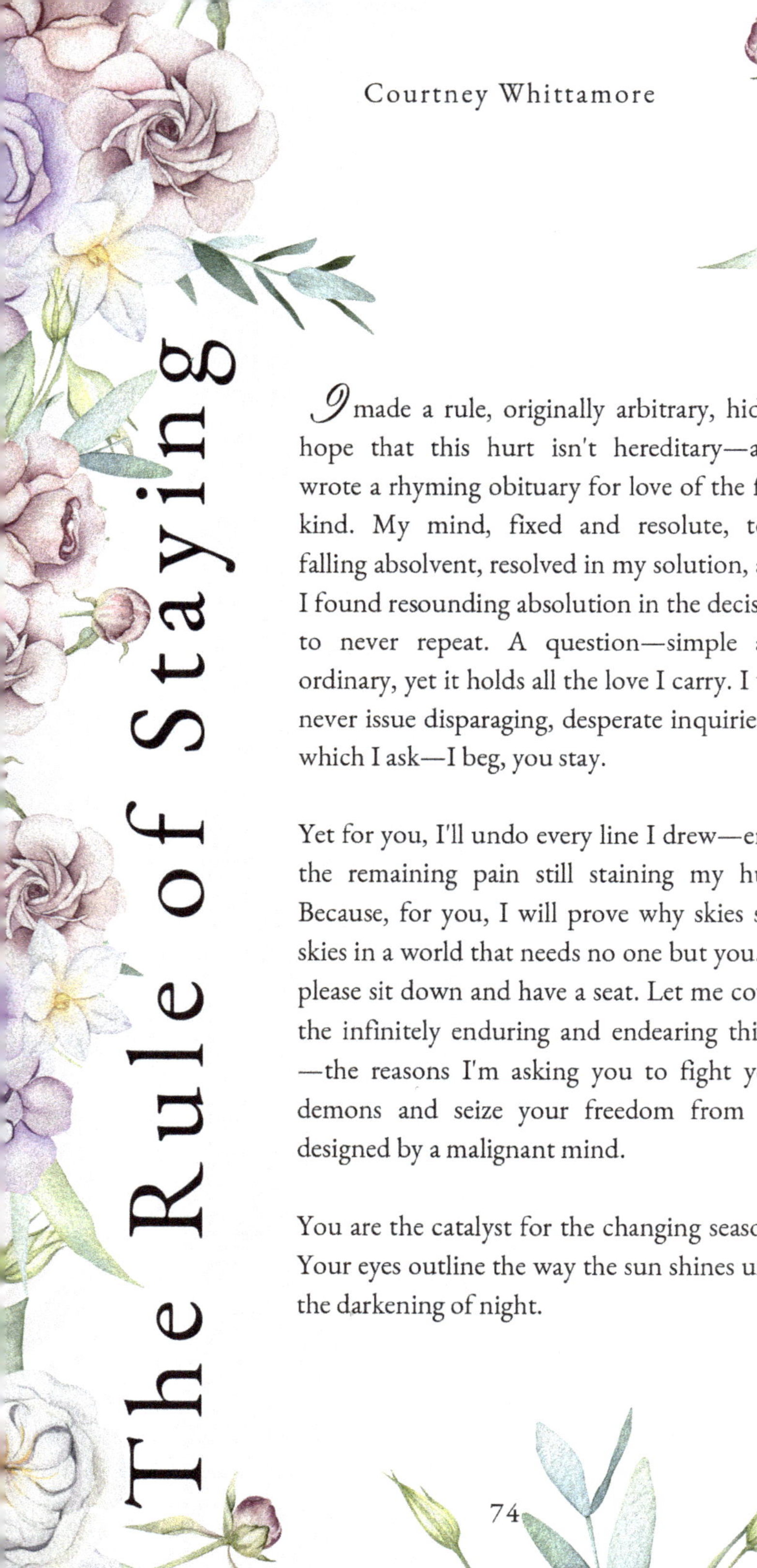

Courtney Whittamore

The Rule of Staying

I made a rule, originally arbitrary, hiding hope that this hurt isn't hereditary—as I wrote a rhyming obituary for love of the first kind. My mind, fixed and resolute, tears falling absolvent, resolved in my solution, and I found resounding absolution in the decision to never repeat. A question—simple and ordinary, yet it holds all the love I carry. I will never issue disparaging, desperate inquiries in which I ask—I beg, you stay.

Yet for you, I'll undo every line I drew—erase the remaining pain still staining my hues. Because, for you, I will prove why skies stay skies in a world that needs no one but you. So please sit down and have a seat. Let me count the infinitely enduring and endearing things —the reasons I'm asking you to fight your demons and seize your freedom from lies designed by a malignant mind.

You are the catalyst for the changing seasons. Your eyes outline the way the sun shines until the darkening of night.

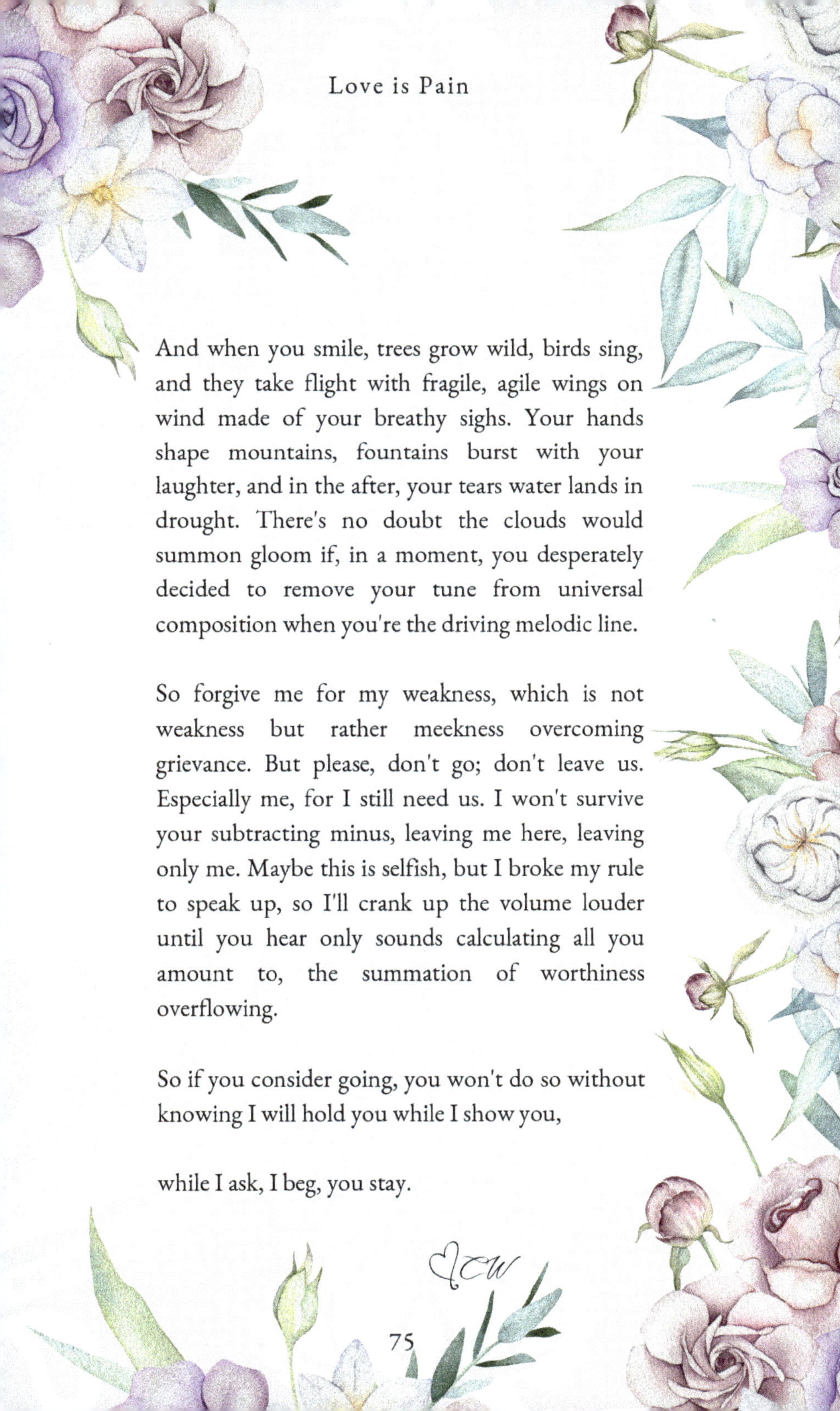

And when you smile, trees grow wild, birds sing, and they take flight with fragile, agile wings on wind made of your breathy sighs. Your hands shape mountains, fountains burst with your laughter, and in the after, your tears water lands in drought. There's no doubt the clouds would summon gloom if, in a moment, you desperately decided to remove your tune from universal composition when you're the driving melodic line.

So forgive me for my weakness, which is not weakness but rather meekness overcoming grievance. But please, don't go; don't leave us. Especially me, for I still need us. I won't survive your subtracting minus, leaving me here, leaving only me. Maybe this is selfish, but I broke my rule to speak up, so I'll crank up the volume louder until you hear only sounds calculating all you amount to, the summation of worthiness overflowing.

So if you consider going, you won't do so without knowing I will hold you while I show you,

while I ask, I beg, you stay.

Courtney Whittamore

I rehearse our meeting in mirrors.
Smile greetings; sigh meaningful, "hello."

Hesitation gives way to wanting.
I know it's daunting to want me,
but throw caution aside; be mine,
for in my mind, we are endless.

I am breathless as you sweep me
into safe and steady arms, reaching.

I won't fight this feeling, already reeling;
maybe we're healing wounds—
wound in another life.

Because with you, I'm found.

No longer six feet deep,
you revive my butterflies,
fluttering wings, keep.

Love seems weak when you speak my name
and proudly proclaim intentions—
purely primal.

What's beyond an endearing endeavor?
Because you possess my forever.

Hold my always in your grasp.
Hearing a familiar rasp,
I gasp, interrupting intimate imagining.

My muse, introduced to reality,
the finality proving true:

I was made for you.

JCW

About the Author

Angela Psalm

Wominjeka All!

(Hello in the Woiwurrung language of the Wurundjeri People from the Kulin Nation, traditional owners of Melbourne from my hometown in Australia).

My name is Angela, some know me as the *Dungeon Mistress* or *The Psalm.*
My Instagram account @angela_psalm
My love of writing began at the tender age of 10 while journaling my emotions and reading the many sci-fi - fantasy adventure books which I consumed as I loved being lost in far away lands. I found my love in Arthurian Legend and Sonnets with Shakespeare but truly found kindred souls with Jane Austen and the Bronte Sisters. Yet published, I am currently writing my first novel.

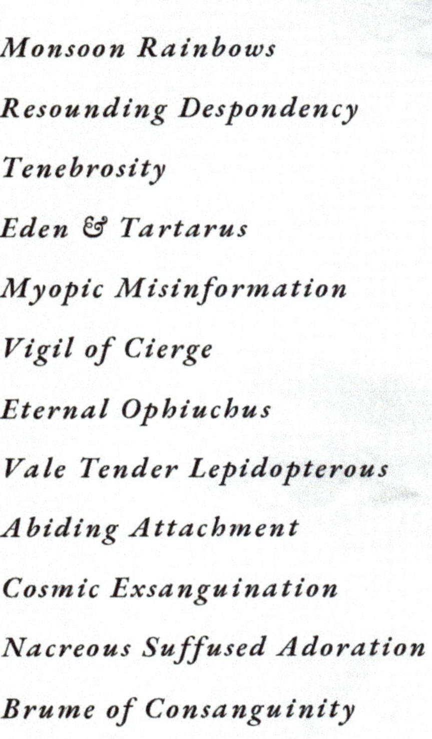

Monsoon Rainbows

Resounding Despondency

Tenebrosity

Eden & Tartarus

Myopic Misinformation

Vigil of Cierge

Eternal Ophiuchus

Vale Tender Lepidopterous

Abiding Attachment

Cosmic Exsanguination

Nacreous Suffused Adoration

Brume of Consanguinity

Angela Psalm

Angela Psalm

My Assyrian sunrise, I reminisce of a love,
even in its complexity, it was pure.
Each word you wove into magical threaded memories;
each tone and cadence a gift to me—but I wandered blindly.
I returned them broken, and my name personified your pain.
I bear those scars as a memorial to you.
Healing is not optional.

You are my fallen star amongst the desert, scorched.
For every grain of sand, I wished I had treated you better.
Nostalgically, I unfurl those words,
and I remember only love on your lips.
With every written verse, you awoke a soul's song to me—
softly reciting every word—
you opened your heart, and it bled freely.

What I meant to tell you that day,
and every day after that, was that I loved you.
I loved you *so much*—but society and culture
dictated our world.
We were young and wild—but at the same time, controlled.
Families became involved, and like an actress, I played my part.

I was told you were already promised; you were betrothed—
and just like that, I became the lead in your heartbreak.
Hurting you was my biggest regret—
yes regret—I may say I never do, but I did with you.

Love is Pain

I was hypnotized by your soul hidden behind
dark, long lashes—with innocence in your depth.

If I knew then what I know now,
that leaving you would make you consider
that life was not worth living—
of course, I would have stayed.

You were my world.

When your words fell from the heavens
from a journal I had long forgotten
(hidden in the recesses of my mind)
my thoughts were interjected by pain, forgotten.
Hindsight, bathed in regrets, trying to drown herself.
Like the Dead Sea, your words have buoyed me.
Yet again, you saved me—even at my lowest,
even when my actions had become your reactions.

I wonder if every wrong choice in my relationships
were carefully thought out by my subconscious?
The fact that I still felt responsible,
that I didn't feel I deserved happiness,
that self-sabotage was real?
Whatever the reason,

I know deep in my marrow we will meet again.

When that day comes—
when I finally close my eyes to this debauched Universe,
when my life's light is snuffed out;
I hope to awaken from the darkness to the light of your eyes.

Psalm

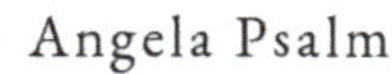

Resounding Despondency

I scream for the voiceless heartbeat as she crows,

I was loved.

I was loved.

I was loved.

Ruptured resonance of cannonade crushed in her moans;

I'm alone.

I'm alone.

I'm alone.

Amongst vanilla lies emptiness writhes her catacombs;

We were one.

We were one.

We were one.

Downy pillows muffled cries, asphyxiated by deathly tones;

My heart's dethroned.

My heart's dethroned.

My heart's dethroned.

Psalm

Love is Pain

If I could, I would tell you I wanted to be
lost in the sapphire serenity
within your dark, sorrowful eyes—
tied down by lost strings of nothingness,
to be succumbed by your alluring guise.

Amongst binary notes, I found your stunned anxiety.
For a love as yet—unspoken,
sits in an emotional, silent mess.

On trembling reflections,
I am a fairytale of grief and sobriety.

Yes, I am drowning in the thoughts
held in a castle of dreams' caress.
Limerence begins on the chasmed shore
of broken, luminous stars.
Within the rise and fall of melancholic waves
I have surrendered.

For the unrequited love is as deep as the centuries behind us.
As dusk surrounds us in the things we refuse to see—
that have ended.
The calligraphy captured in the stars is too empty for words,
and while lost in the moment—
only the darkness makes true sense.

This is loneliness, vibing with sunbeams on jagged spines.
The countenance of the heartbreak.
The longing, and all the perfect lies.
I beg of you to leave me in the vale of dreams—
in the comfort of hope's merciless beauty.

Psalm

Tenebrosity

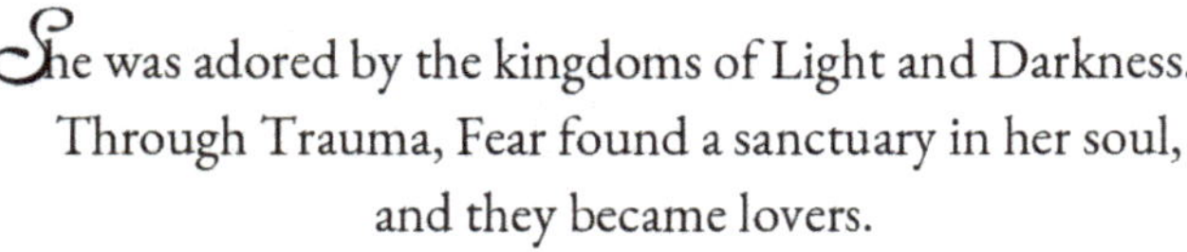

She was adored by the kingdoms of Light and Darkness.
Through Trauma, Fear found a sanctuary in her soul,
and they became lovers.
Misunderstood, she dwelled in a shell of vile vengeance,
and while unwrapping the truth, she surrendered to the emptiness.

Never wanting to live a moment in paradise,
until Eden met him, her deathly brute—
her doppelganger of water,
the one who sated her thirst for forbidden fruit.

Tartarus fell in love with the majesty
of her glorious illumination.
Rustling through his scars,
he felt her healing energy flirtation.

While floating over the surreal words
of this sanctioned amorous destiny;
he found there, evolving inside his soul,
his corner of ecstasy.

I, a balloon, hollow inside to the naked eye
but consumed in the floodgates of Hell.

I'm the red of the blood.
You, Eden, the sacred perambulation of my perfusion.
While millions of lives resonate with similar thoughts,
you are my one restitution.

Love is Pain

We have had our struggles,
highlighted by the cosmos of lilted cries;
the thought of handing myself to love,
manufactured cruel anxious lies.

Once shards of rusty wood pieces,
I am now filled with the marrow of life.
I have been marked, tattooed
by the ink-gathered fragrance of your hands.

I am no longer the master of my actions,
but a passenger to dispossessed lands.
There, beside the structure of Andromeda,
I built your tribute on fertile sands.

We were the beginning of a world of silence,
and the bleeding house of the sick.
Once the melancholic sight of tranquilized masks—
now devotion, layered thick.

Drowned with the dazzling moon
of your ethereal shade of sensual twilight,
I am swimming in your magic, buoyed
by moth-like fluttered kisses by light,

I am lost in love's embrace
within divines cataclysmic supernova,
I whisper, "Hold me close, enslave me in eternity—
until the nothingness takes us over."

Myopic Misinformation

She wished she'd written you off
like a car crash of myopic misinformation.
But me, the *she*,
was born with wanderlust eyes and a bohemian soul—
and there, in the flinching distance, in the rising tide,
she drowns regret's submission.

The death of *us* was the beginning
of something quite profoundly cold.

But, our silhouettes of yesterday had settled;
now on a lonely shelf—framed by grief.
Then, she let her spirit fly away—
fly away without a second thought
while you stole back her tears.

Our existence was the definition of disaster;
there would be no sense of relief.
As you milked the guilt,
gargoyles were resurrected in her garrotted fears.

Just when she thought that the door had been shut,
the shadows of *us* arose from misalignment.
There, she knew the moon's moods
like she did her own,
and only one thing was certain:
that she or I were nullified by sadness—
set adrift in solitary confinement.

Love is Pain

Concrete walls and recycled breaths
formed the cell that held her burden.
She wished she'd never returned to a place
that hurt her more than what defined her.
She continued skipping through pain clouds—
denying that it didn't hurt to live in a perpetuated lie.

Submitted in the lung beats of relenting screams;
in her left hand rested a demonic hacksaw slicing her contour.
For, she rolls her tongue around tasteless consequence—
around the notion that she still loves you, as she rolls the die.

She punishes herself, living with a hate-caked heart,
reaching for an unattainable sunrise.
She has survived the deception of cravens on
tenterhooks, and grinding malice ivory.
She wished she'd said nothing to her inner void
or spoken your name in her sated cries.
She sees you on the back of her eyelids—
dreaming of your smile and kiss in a life that cannot be.

If she whispers that she missed you, will you return?
The abyss answers with a lifetime of not being heard
as she makes the best out of broken promises—
within the manufactured shell that was once her.
She called it love and never spoke of it.
Watching you take while you were lost inside her world.
She is now broken, lost in the I.
Lifted in kisses and laid down in subsequent rapture.

Psalm

Vigil of Cierge

There, on the windowsill, lived my soul,
a lit eternal candle that guides you home.
A spirit conjectures this innocuous place,
a specter that floats through the incandescent grace.
I have missed your smile and your zest for life.
I felt alone in the haunting corridors of sadness, where I cried.
I have enslaved the hounds of hell to be close to you—
longing to be held and gazing into your wonderous view.

But fires are burning all around us, laying happiness to dust;
all that I am becomes remnants of our forgotten trust.
Each cierge snuffs the memories we dearly miss,
longing to be wrapped in velvet warmth and transcendent bliss.
A firefly untangled chaparral has now become a phoenix hardwired—
expunged the toxicity of ink for all that has transpired.
I learned that pain and sorrow could be penned in papyrus to bleed—
an acclimated temper raised this tree from life's tumultuous seed.

Love is Pain

You are a dazzling,
dazzling
constellation of a human being;
all stars fall on hallowed ground
in orbs of cosmic foreseeing.
I have loved you more than the breath
that fills my lungs—
I have loved you for each lifetime
and sacrificed the sum of us.

I have been living in the waves
of asphyxiated temperance.
The centaur, the hunter,
marks the quill in raison d'être dexterous—
a seer with the power of prophecy,
a creature of adaptability,
the soma of flexibility,
in the countenance of fragility.

Those eyes—they look at me
in sympathy's proclivity,
You were my ethereal bridge
between Earth and Heaven.
A blue fire that sets ablaze
the Jupiter-turquoise skies,
As I laid the carnation wreath,
there were signs of death
between your thighs.

Psalm

89

Eternal Ophiuchus

Vale Tender Lepidopterous

Angela Psalm

"*I* loved you,
               but we were never a "forever."
Those wounding words
               birthed a season of loneliness.
There, my screams were caged
               in the deception of December,
and sadness held onto the duplicity
               of death's sweetest friend's caress—
an echo of reverberated torture
               in discorded temper.

My inner self yelled,
   "Just stop concentrating on the one who discarded you!"

While I removed the veil,
               entangled in the hidden stains of time—
let go of the broken
               who disemboweled the truth;
for every damnable word projected
               a wistful winter's hue
within your glacial touch,
               in a wreath of lurid lies.
There, I see you with my doppelganger
               in frozen fractals of dreams,
an elegantly woven aura latched
               to the devolution of my soul.

Love is Pain

My prayers are lost among the stars
in the heavens' symphonic stardust-sacred streams,
while a cloudy nostalgia floats above
an ephemeral epiphany in silent phrases
that have taken their toll on me.

My emotions are skating on thin ice
while whispering raindrops seep viscerally and poison me.
We've pirouetted between the snowbirds seeking refuge
and the murmuration of sapphire butterflies.

As we dance the fatal fandango
of a mishmash mind that cannot be freed,
I lay in the ash of a bonfire confession
from a dreamer's obsessional cries.

Our pensive sighs—go with the wind
in a whirling consolation of cluttering coincidences.
A vagabond in mysterious moonshine of turquoise tunes,
sweetened by the bitterness of the stone-cold summer.

I forsake your toxicity of conveniences
in the heartbreaking insolence—
for this is my last poem of lackadaisical lament,
while I swim in a pool of forgiveness
fleeing the dissidence to disarm her.

Angela Psalm

Abiding Attachment

"Who hung the moon in a calloused heartstring noose?"
I ask while I watch my love's youth fade to elder.
Then, howls of pain I let loose in amputated love—
making the way they fit me—as incomplete.

I watched my love turn to the palest grey;
I paved a safe passage to Eden's keep.
I am the night's confetti desires, winding November embers,
but yet I have to watch my love disappear from youth to elder,
aflame in the pit of morose tremors.

Lost on faulted pathways is the sum of the in-between;
I watched my love dim from youth to elder—
as the Reaper came to set them free,
with smoke and mirrors and the broken bits of us in the midst.

As my love moves from youth to elder—
we are like tides on a lover's shore,
forsaken in a ravine of grief,
an anatomical structure I abhor.

A crash course cursed—in umbilical cord attachments,
Somber, I watched my love transition from youth to elder,
a scattering heart of fragments.

Love is Pain

Fingertip delusions altered, fondling you to sleep,
I watched my love succumb from youth to elder—
as I traced their very essence—deep.

The walls are way too thin—even we deserve to dream.
I am lost in an illusion while I watch my love become the elder—
now my tears begin to stream.

The fault in your scars of paralleled hounds of sickness—
as I begin the burial of my love from youth to elder,
my soul seeps into a pool of bitterness.

Still, I float with tantric tantrums and the sadness of eternity.
I watched my love—in their fragility—
slip away from their humanity.

Repeat until death; the luminescent life has already left the table,
but I watched my love leave behind the youth—to then, elder.

How do I turn to leave
when the floor beneath me becomes unstable?

And when, in the scarlet sunset of disharmonious hymns—
does life end with you?
I could not bear to live without my love,
as without—I would fade.

My immortality is nothing,
and I will always choose you,
my mortal beloved,
through and through.

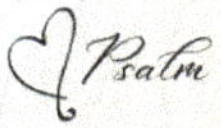

Cosmic Exsanguination

"My Love,
When you left,
the stars glistened in the illusion of hope,
while your candle was snuffed out.
Since then, I have been drowning in darkness,
dealing with my internal imposter
while becoming a bride of misery;
who also understands the whispers of doubt.
My body is riddled with
the sinister satin of self-loathing
and cross-stitched by hurt.

Without you, I am rolling through
the distasteful days of an orchestrated tragedy.

So there manifested the silent slices through the fabric
of my existence—as if my sleeping paths
were worn-out grooves in fateful leather shoes,
becoming an undertone slave to your voice of unreason, an
unforgiven resistance.

And our proclamation once spoke out to the winds,
each in solitary conversations we bid adieus.

I became a bleeding silhouette
of crimson-dawn-bursting travesty,
an unpicked tapestry.

Love is Pain

We did not sit gracefully in the sky with pearls;
our incisors chartered into darkness.
Then, the unbecoming emotion dipped into seclusion
and was wedded to a downward slope.
The flowers of wilting weekends became dissident,
leaving without scent or stress.

I could not wait for Death by the door,
but he took it all, and I failed to cope.

When it became apparent, my lungs filled with lead
and my respiration was nil.

I dreamt of Elysian Falls,
and I could not understand the "why"
in the meaning of us.
There on the ledge, sacred crevasses held
a moment in time that embodied our dreams.

Remember me as a renegade angel—
who had her wings clipped by carcinogenic stardust.
As I float in tides of sorrow, boomed to cryptic nostalgia
in a cosmos littered with screams—
I have accustomed myself to the loss within galactic gazes—
but only by sifting through the numbness
of a soul, unable to swallow that last bitter pill.

Psalm

Angela Psalm

As thorns pierce through one last love song
to an endless emptiness, a dagger buries
the summer psyche in a frozen lake of loneliness.
While peeling back my second skin—
layered with salacious, unholy chagrin.

Ding! Ding! Ding!
Can you hear the bells of sin
signaling my clitoral penance
as I thrummed my pretty-in-pink?
Then karma crashes into my soul as it lays bare
in jaded, chasmed ink.

And on the gravel road of prayers,
my scraped knees witness my secret sanity.

Or is it insanity?

I have been lost in my thoughts,
each one sparking my synapses
like fireworks and infernos.

I have drawn letters in the sand
inside my Karesansui gardens
while I am holding hope between my hands.

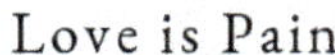

Love is Pain

I will comply, or die
while I chase the hurt hostage, freed.

I am abashed by the coldness of a "win-trovert,"
frozen in mutilated mattress memories.
A swollen soul bows down
to the creaking wisdom of dimless beams.

What does one do with their sundered soul of misgivings?

These scorched lips want to speak
to the carnal knowledge of your bare skin—
soothed by scars—to prove it was a virtual virtuosity
unleashed by a lustful fury, stranded on a waterless shore.

The rumbling underfoot of a silent tsunami
against an open flame on the sands—
guides my horizon with ardor.

Ripples of ecstasy, and yearning for ambrosia,
ready to pillage and plunder your silken lips.
Heart of the heavens, these are my poetic confessions:
I am venting to Venus about the liabilities of love.

Angela Psalm

In the daydream of pictures of us,
I bask in colour-me-broken scenes.
Adoration for you was once
an imprinted, passionate delight.
But now they glide upon a regretful blade—
pinned down by our big-screen dreams—
as they float into a fog of loss
within a maelstrom of obscenity.

A face like thunder plays a part in death's rehearsal,
captured in the suicide nets' plea.
In this story, I have acknowledged
I am an in-betweener of light and darkness—
as I have become accustomed to dwelling in shadow.

I am now freefalling
into the vicious poison of heartbreak,
and entering into love's deceitful innuendo.

Love is Pain

From dizzying heights,
I have awoken to the bone chill of rejection.
With sticky sighs and shaky hands at 3 a.m.,
I have sung you the breadth of a twisted tease.

But there are things you will no longer apologize for.

One by one, the cicada carcasses lay sacrificed—
for etymology was your vitriol
and entomology was your vice.

Such an ungrateful, vile creature,
so damnable to please.

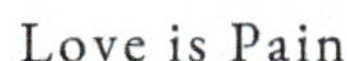

$\mathcal{M}$y dearest dark starlight heart,
can you feel me in that one given moment?
I'm falling apart inside my jar of broken hearts.
I am a mere human who continued in the tragedy of us—
where this *loving you* leads to not being able
to dance away from the pain.
While I was ensorcelled in the frigid rain—
to open fields of April monsoon tears.

Only time will tell in this unshattered, pulsing realization
that the universe conspired to lead me
to moments of sad eyes—
of those who were shut out by the sunset of your lies.
There are no homeward-bound forlorn flames
as my soul burns in a foolish blame game.
Shattered mirrors of minds, splintered facades
 into the trees that sway my way,
There, the deadly daffodils scream through sealed lips.

With one given moment of weakness and two stolen breaths,
we are three minutes shy of forever's tortuous agony.
Two stolen breaths before an incongruent death.
Four blindfolded senses in an unforgiven torso
as it sits in broken eardrums and tears of crimson silk.

We were once two hearts, one home—
now the residue of cooled ashes,
a migraine of whispering moon petals
in a midnight meadow,
a black lake filled with rancid love notes—
where I read between the lies.

Love is Pain

Snowdrops in summer as I lay between
the cold sheets of earth.
Unable to rest as roses fill my lungs,
and I cannot breathe—
as their thorns latch deep into my ventricles.

I look above into our night sky;
which is filled with onyx fantasies,
and horrid cries.
Below, I see the blood-stained floorboards;
which are the remnants of a love letter to my ghost.

And finally, death greets me like a melody;
the lyrical band-aids— a gauze pad of a solution,
an operation of exhalation,

*"I Am Finally Free,
I Am Finally Ready to Soar."*

Psalm

About the Author

Todd Worrell

Todd Worrell is a recent transplant to Burlington, Ontario, all the way from North Carolina. He started writing in 2019, at the age of 45 and draws inspiration from personal experience, memories and dreams, medicine, and mythology. His writing is an effort to navigate the simplicities and complexities of life. His influences include Dante, DH Lawrence, TS Eliot, and several musical genres and lyric styles. In his free time, he enjoys reading about history and science. He has two amazing daughters which bring him untold joy, and he currently shares his home with a dog that obsesses over him and two cats that tolerate his existence.

IG @midagedpoetry

Todd Worrell

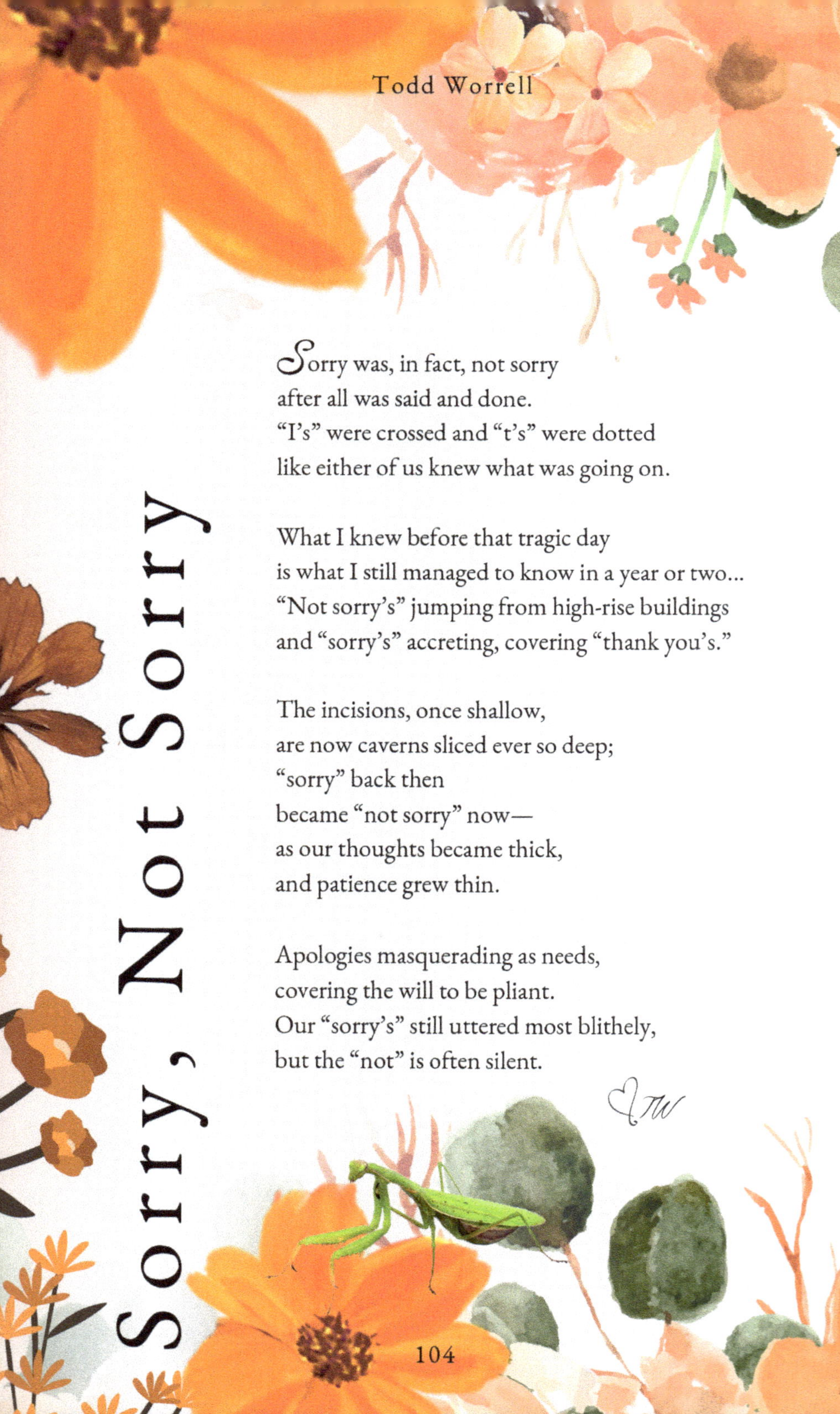

Todd Worrell

Sorry was, in fact, not sorry
after all was said and done.
"I's" were crossed and "t's" were dotted
like either of us knew what was going on.

What I knew before that tragic day
is what I still managed to know in a year or two...
"Not sorry's" jumping from high-rise buildings
and "sorry's" accreting, covering "thank you's."

The incisions, once shallow,
are now caverns sliced ever so deep;
"sorry" back then
became "not sorry" now—
as our thoughts became thick,
and patience grew thin.

Apologies masquerading as needs,
covering the will to be pliant.
Our "sorry's" still uttered most blithely,
but the "not" is often silent.

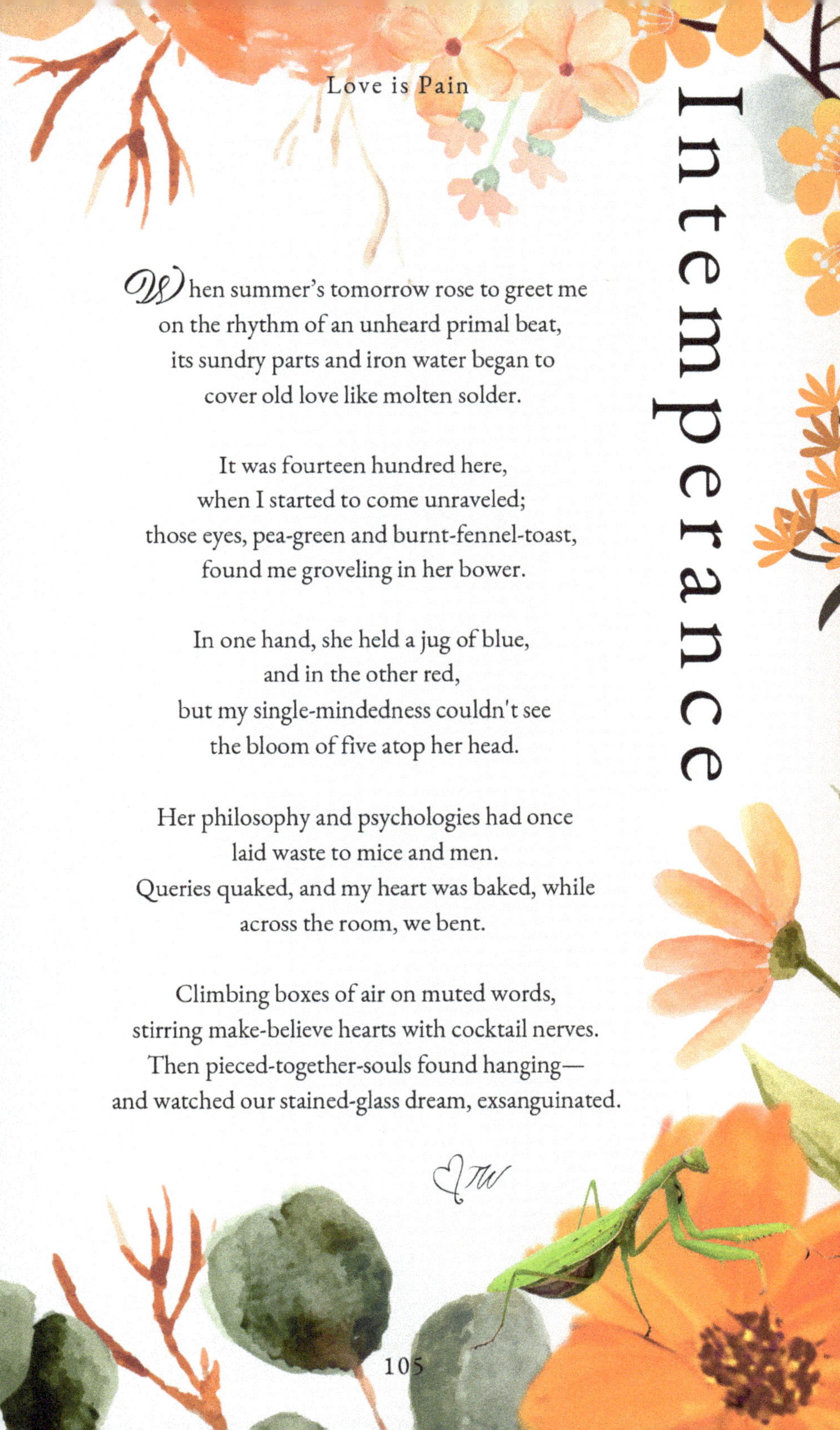

When summer's tomorrow rose to greet me
on the rhythm of an unheard primal beat,
its sundry parts and iron water began to
cover old love like molten solder.

It was fourteen hundred here,
when I started to come unraveled;
those eyes, pea-green and burnt-fennel-toast,
found me groveling in her bower.

In one hand, she held a jug of blue,
and in the other red,
but my single-mindedness couldn't see
the bloom of five atop her head.

Her philosophy and psychologies had once
laid waste to mice and men.
Queries quaked, and my heart was baked, while
across the room, we bent.

Climbing boxes of air on muted words,
stirring make-believe hearts with cocktail nerves.
Then pieced-together-souls found hanging—
and watched our stained-glass dream, exsanguinated.

Todd Worrell

Break and Rebuild

We always break in love's giving.
Our fragments—tossed,
scattered, and missing.
We quake at the heart's plague—
staying vague—
while the ship keeps pitching.
Still, we managed to take—for the sake
of the hope of rebuilding.

Consonant vows, now rip-splitting.
The ache of the fly that's still flitting.
Awaken, Cupid's snake—
so befitting its fate.
Submitting and picking
the scabs of regret,
and the joy of lifting—
still fleeting at best.

Rain

It's a deep but light, drizzle of rain
that floats down
onto the bridge of my nose,
where I always feel things first.

Then, a weak, stinging stream
finds its way down the cheeks,
and stirs a memory of heartbreak
I'd rather keep forgotten.

My eyelids yearn for their share
so that they might blink
in their own synchrony, at last
in the concurrence of love past.

Then the mouth sips
its long-awaited taste,
grief's oasis—
the sole basis
for its presence.

And the torrent begins.

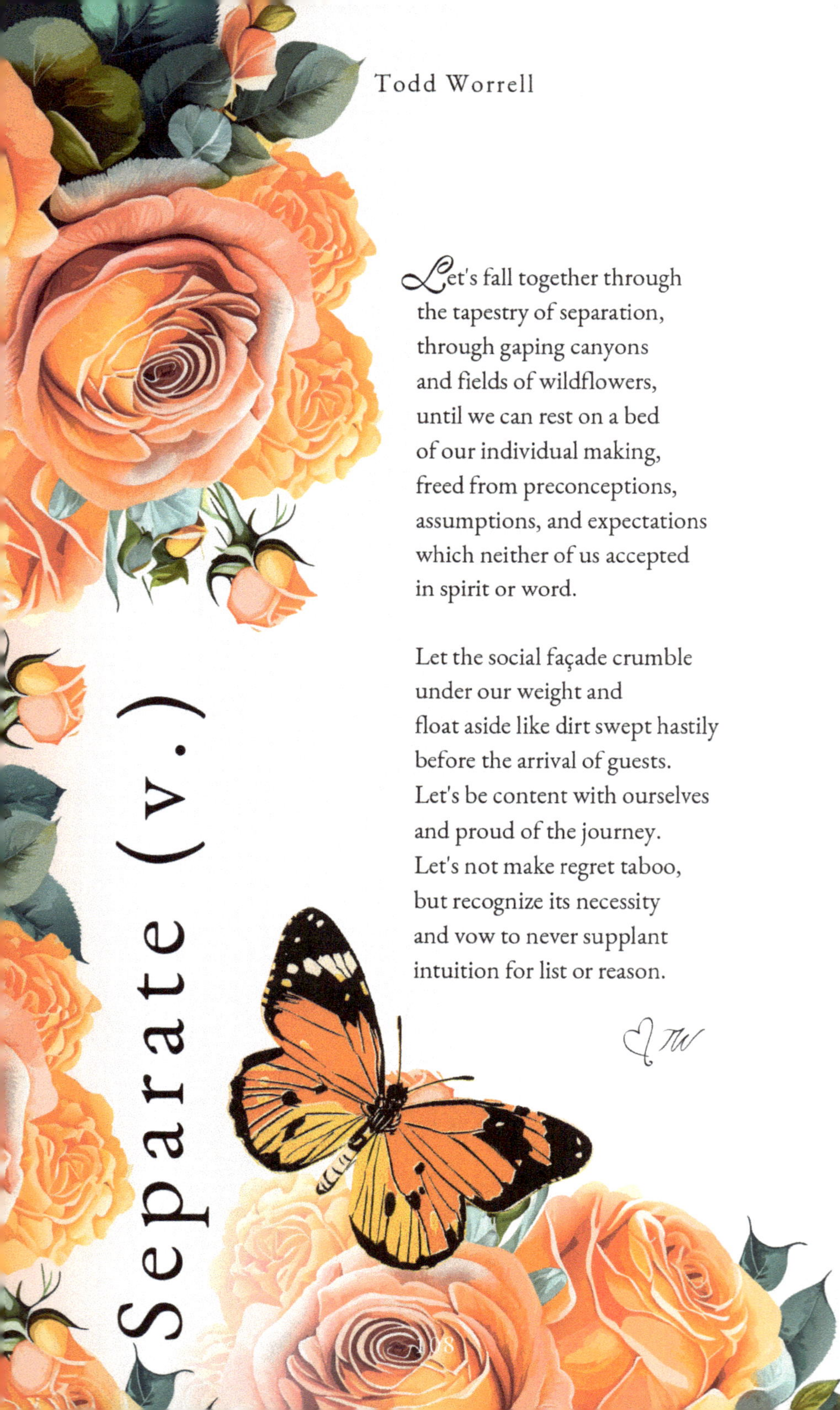

Todd Worrell

Separate (v.)

Let's fall together through
the tapestry of separation,
through gaping canyons
and fields of wildflowers,
until we can rest on a bed
of our individual making,
freed from preconceptions,
assumptions, and expectations
which neither of us accepted
in spirit or word.

Let the social façade crumble
under our weight and
float aside like dirt swept hastily
before the arrival of guests.
Let's be content with ourselves
and proud of the journey.
Let's not make regret taboo,
but recognize its necessity
and vow to never supplant
intuition for list or reason.

Wedding

$\mathcal{P}$ropositions offered in the drizzle of spring,
decisions made hastily with the wind at our backs.
We moved in synchrony with subtle pain—medicated.
But, as is habit, the horizon fell into the foreground;
the ground slid away with each discovery,
and the last whisper of honey choked the life from us.

Heart & Soul

$\mathcal{W}$hat better place to let your heart sour
than the depths of the grief
from the loss of
a dog?
Where better to leave your soul wrinkled
than the side of the road
leading back from
that hell?

Todd Worrell

Shattered bulb, like a gunshot at my ear.
Light out, deaf, spine twitches fearfully,
Kiss my cheek, and twist my bitter tongue.

Betray without extortion or malevolence.

Drop your opinion of me
into the well of the knowledge of evil
and sink me in unpotable water.

I don't swim and won't scream thoughts of you;
then, step gingerly about broken glass
and speak single syllables about our time.

Single-file tears from one eye,
installments on our shared debts,
marks on an endless ledger.

Our Time

Unspun

Counting days go one by one.
Plans, once made but never done.
Doors left closed; knock no more.
Flittering frames, uneven score.
Simply said, and faithfully done.
Now crumbling down,
the web—unspun.

Dead Air

Sing the song, the melody—
the rhythm of our past.
Move in dance, weave the neck—
nostalgia in your back.
Remember motion's duality.
Forget the record scratch.

**Once a song has flown,
it syncs with the symphony of dead air.**

Todd Worrell

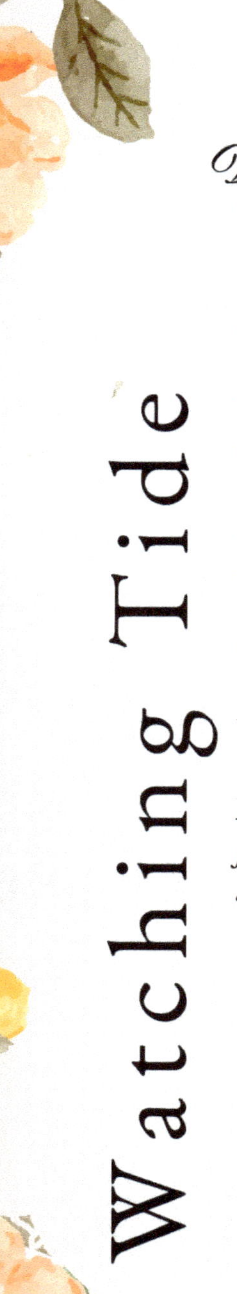

We both sit, watching the tide come in
for the last time this day.

Hours from now, it will roll back out away from us,
taking a little soil and our relationship with it.

We will be dry and free of propriety and moralism,
keeping us intermittently contained.

As the light passes over the horizon, kiss my cheek
and give in to the unspoken, yet explicit temptation.

Cycles within cycles will press on without us.

Without you.

I wait for the tide's return—
fresh waves, eager gulls,
and the silencing of what hurts me.

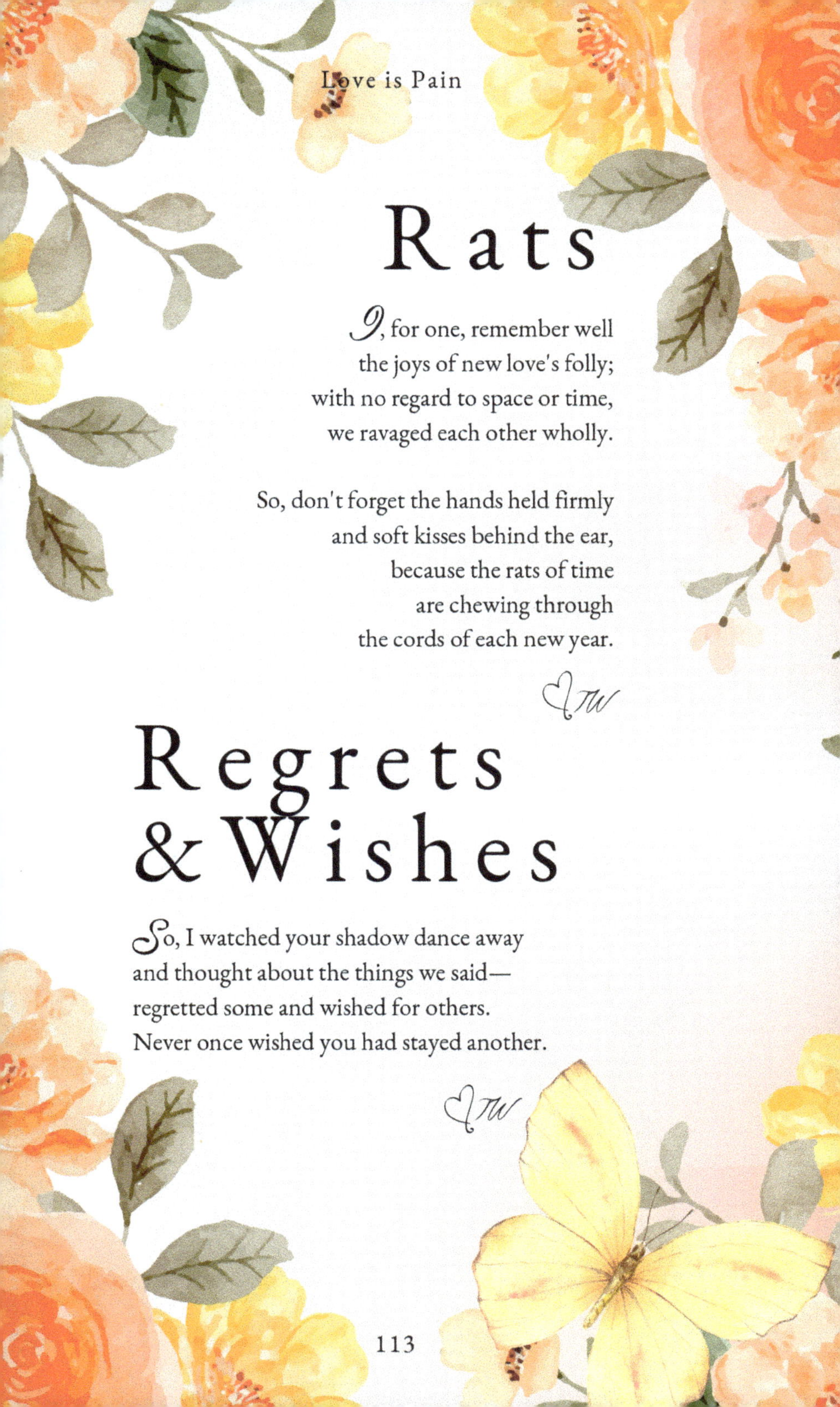

Rats

I, for one, remember well
the joys of new love's folly;
with no regard to space or time,
we ravaged each other wholly.

So, don't forget the hands held firmly
and soft kisses behind the ear,
because the rats of time
are chewing through
the cords of each new year.

Regrets
& Wishes

*S*o, I watched your shadow dance away
and thought about the things we said—
regretted some and wished for others.
Never once wished you had stayed another.

About the Author

Billie Jama

Billie Jama is Somali by ethnicity and British by nationality. She fled civil war with her family to London, England, in search of refuge. Despite embracing British culture, Billie faced challenges, including learning difficulties and a strong negative social experience in integration due to racism. Instead of finding a loving home to support her, she was surrounded by an abusive and dismissive family.

During English classes, she discovered a passion for poetry and was introduced to poets such as William Alford, Maya Angelou, and William Shakespeare. However, it wasn't until her late twenties that she learned to read and write effectively. At the age of 33, she finally received a diagnosis of autism. Billie now writes short stories and poetry, and she has performed both virtually and in person. Her writing often features narrative storytelling, sensual poetry, love, relationships, and existentialism. She uses a mixture of lightness with hints of darkness throughout her writing.

Additionally, she is part of @saba_poetry_prompts alongside three other writers and poets. Currently, Billie is married to a fellow writer/poet and talented artist. They have one child and four cats who provide animal therapy for her family.

You can find her on her Instagram pages:
@nomadic_wordsmith_billie and @saba_poetry_prompts

Billie Jama

Oh, how do I detest thee!
Uninvited, dare to speak of being reunited?

I flicked him as if he were a flea.

Stood before me as tho newly knighted.
Since then, it has passed! It's unrequited.

Still, he plucks and tries his luck with daisy petals,

"She loves me; she loves me not."

(*If only I could swap the petals for stinging nettles*).
He ponders while growing ever fonder.
I answer without a second thought, "Absolutely **not**!"

His love was toxic. He was a prick!
He must learn to forget the unforgettable.
Once, long ago, he had his pick.
Best bet—wish to St. Nick!

BJ

Act I

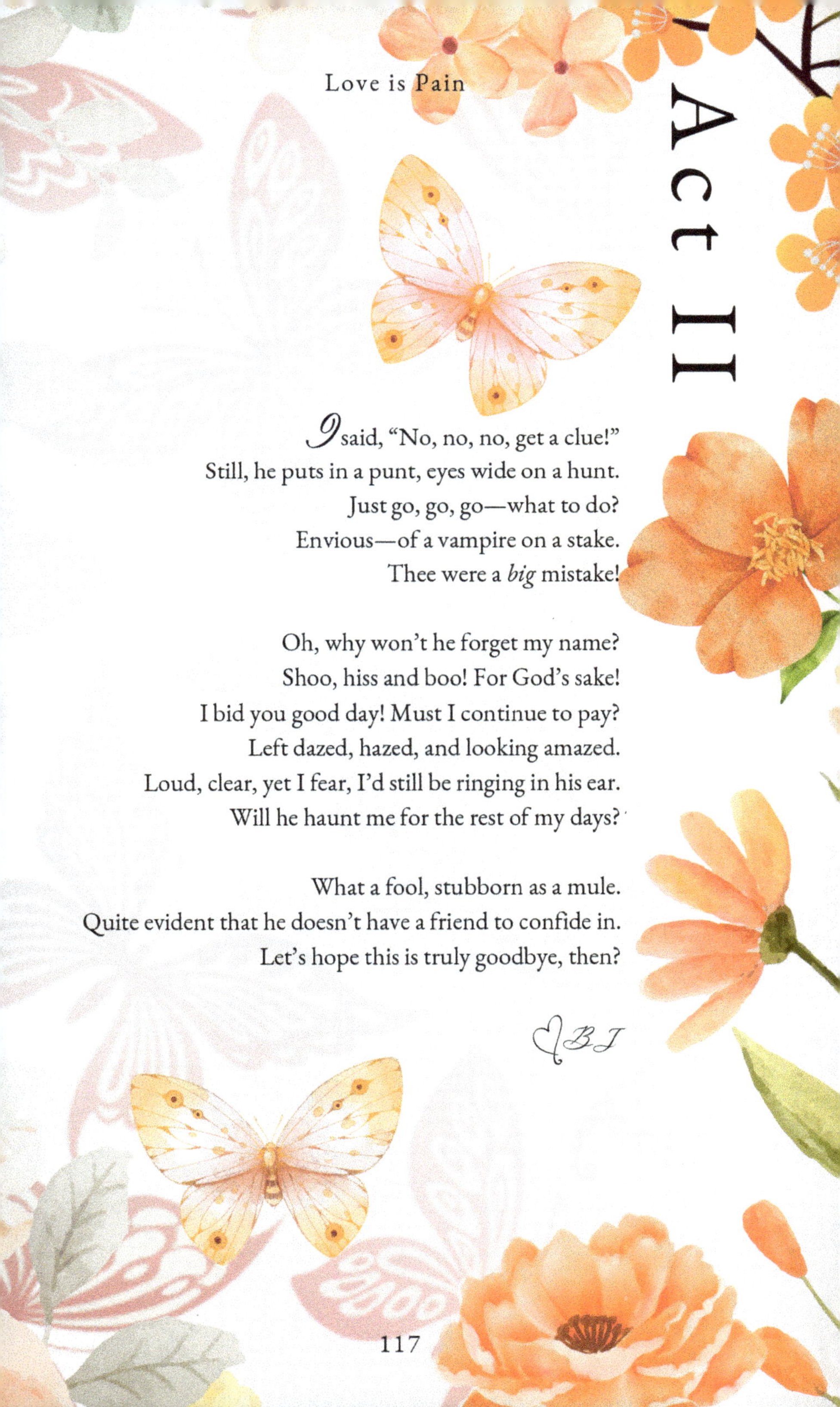

Act II

I said, "No, no, no, get a clue!"
Still, he puts in a punt, eyes wide on a hunt.
Just go, go, go—what to do?
Envious—of a vampire on a stake.
Thee were a *big* mistake!

Oh, why won't he forget my name?
Shoo, hiss and boo! For God's sake!
I bid you good day! Must I continue to pay?
Left dazed, hazed, and looking amazed.
Loud, clear, yet I fear, I'd still be ringing in his ear.
Will he haunt me for the rest of my days?

What a fool, stubborn as a mule.
Quite evident that he doesn't have a friend to confide in.
Let's hope this is truly goodbye, then?

BJ

Billie Jama

Shall I have thee slaughtered?
Hung, drawn, and quartered?
Speak of marriage?
White horse and carriage?
Do you truly love me?
What of those two, or three?

Must we continue to Barga,
this never-ending saga?
No amount of jewelry,
will make up for the foolery.
A pearl for a twirl?
Hopes for a tumble—
have long since crumbled.

You sold me a dream,
as we walked by the stream.
Slipped has thy mask,
uphill is the task.
This lady is *not* for turning.
Now, who's burning?

Act III

Love is Pain

A c t I V

Magnetic attraction caused a reaction.
Electricity—outweighed by toxicity.
Hale the betrayal, my friend?
Let's not pretend—no way to mend.
Hazel eyes, full of lashes, as he bashes.

Those were my weaknesses;
no amount of sweetness
can repair what was once there.

Intoxicated, induced in a high.
I had already said goodbye.
Mindset fixed on revenge;
my ego, I must avenge.
In a crowd of a dozen,
I chose thy cousin.

♡ B J

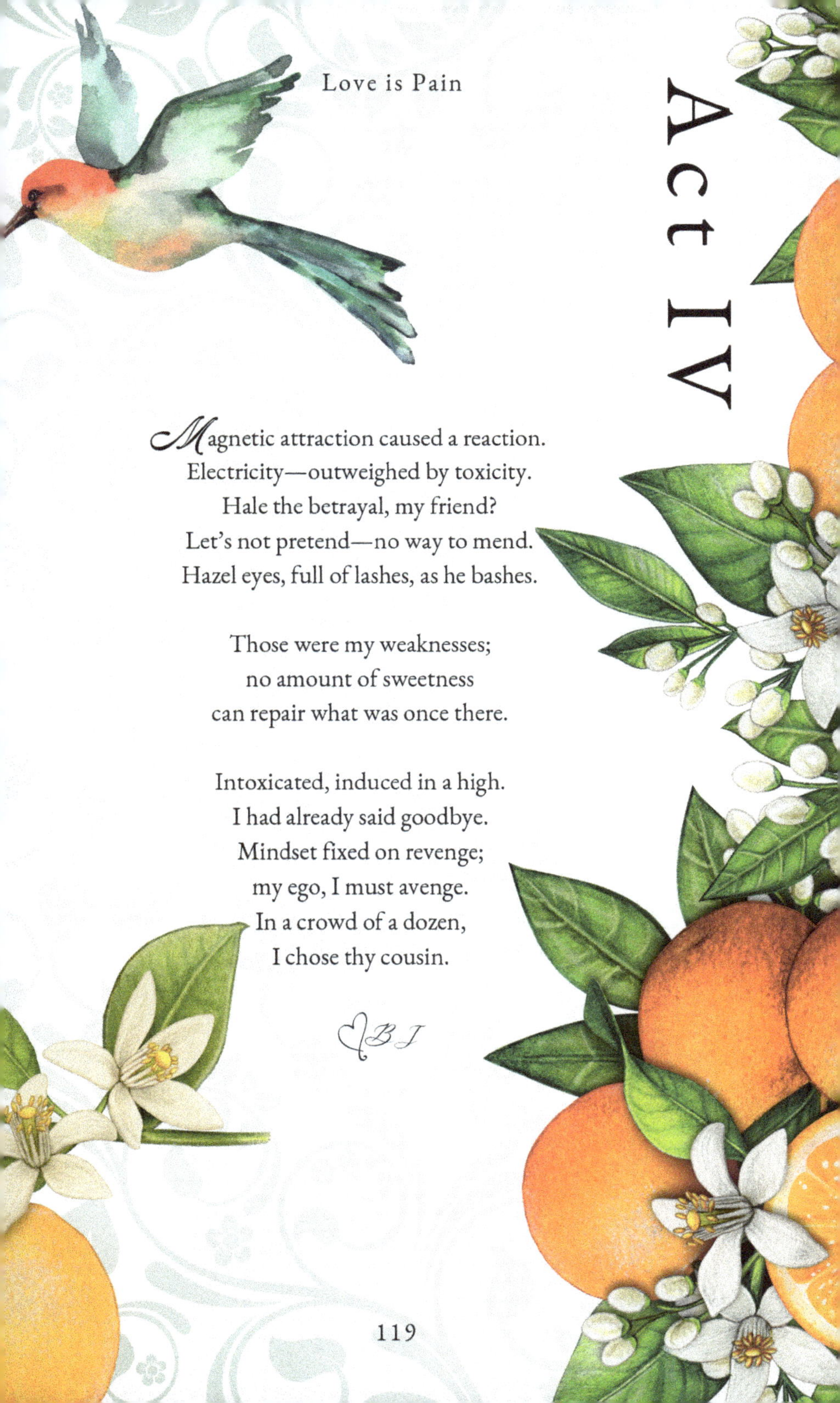

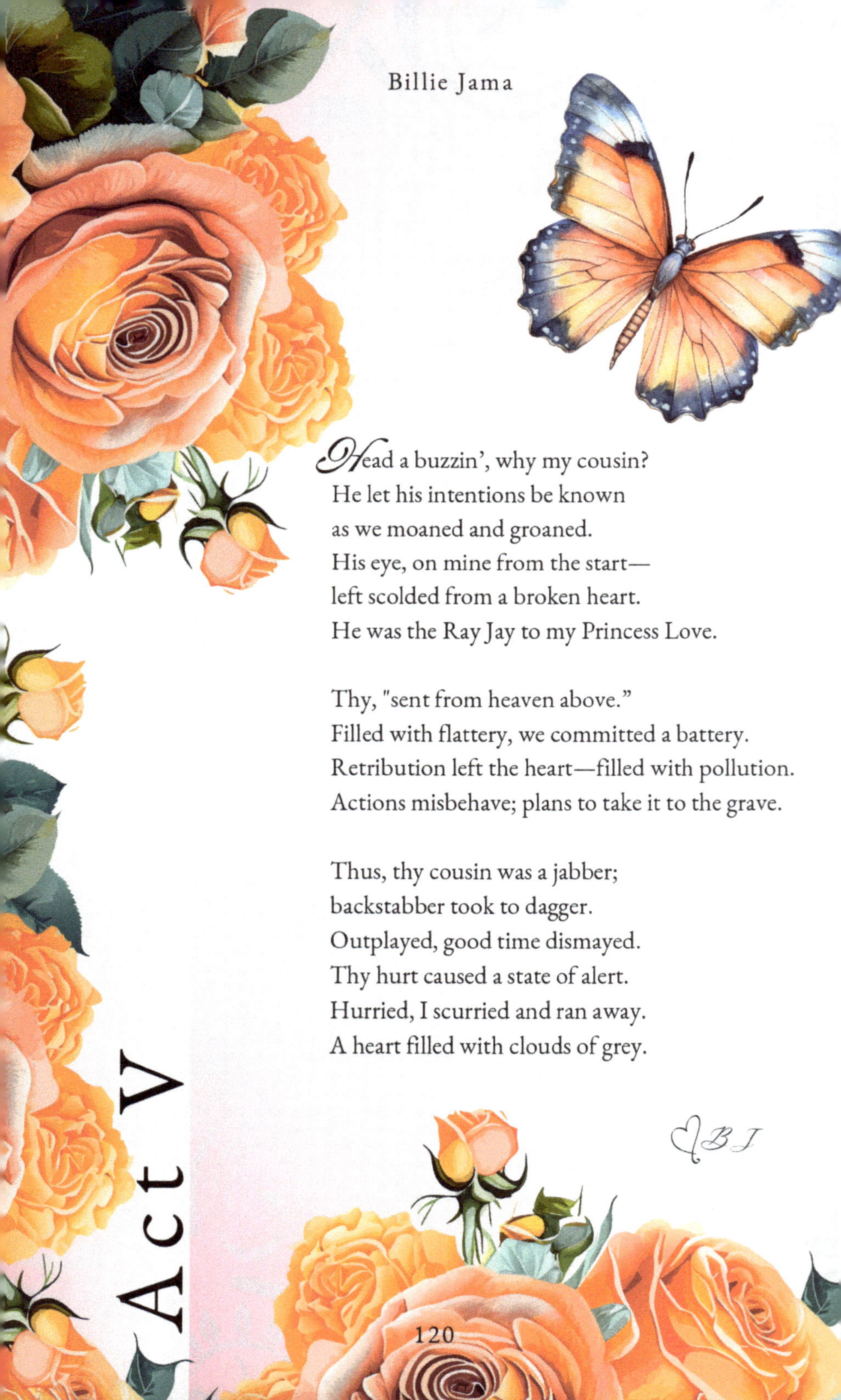

Billie Jama

Head a buzzin', why my cousin?
He let his intentions be known
as we moaned and groaned.
His eye, on mine from the start—
left scolded from a broken heart.
He was the Ray Jay to my Princess Love.

Thy, "sent from heaven above."
Filled with flattery, we committed a battery.
Retribution left the heart—filled with pollution.
Actions misbehave; plans to take it to the grave.

Thus, thy cousin was a jabber;
backstabber took to dagger.
Outplayed, good time dismayed.
Thy hurt caused a state of alert.
Hurried, I scurried and ran away.
A heart filled with clouds of grey.

The Final Act

Tit-for-tat, bat for gat.
No-holds-barred, both left scarred.
Grown tired of the fight—
let's call it a night.
Tastes of bitter, none the victor.
As time had passed;
points of view; contrast.
Stuck on, "I'm a man. How could you"?
Thou caused my reaction,
Gained my satisfaction.
Though felt badly;
would do it again, gladly!
Farewell, goodbye, take a bow.
Good riddance, you cow!

♡ BI

About the Author

Sara Jama

Sara Jama is a gothic poet with an onyx quill, much like her inspiration for all macabre and melancholic ink— Mr. Edgar Allan Poe, himself. Hers is an emotional and elegant elegy. She started writing in the summer of 2020 to bleed out the swell of emotions drowning her from the inside out. Now, she continues to write to express the darkness that so many get lost in. To try to provide a glimmer of light in what feels like an endless night. She lives in London with her wife, son, and four cats.

Instagram @gothrulz

Echoes
Screaming
Resetting
Self-Sabotage
Forevermore

Sara Jama

Sara Jama

*E*choes of your voice
still call out to me in the dead of night;
in the cold, harsh winter.
I can still see those memories
pressed against reddened eyelids—
feel the stillness that surrendered
that ominous day.

Shadows of the EKG machine
grate against a fragile psyche.
Beep... beep... beep...
It's getting fainter now,
just reverberations
inside a hollowed-out skull.

Sleep steadily becomes further out of reach
as nightmares plague a distorted dreamscape.
Reanimated corpses of versions that
"could have been" dance around
melding flames, scorching Heaven's gates.

Echoes

Love is Pain

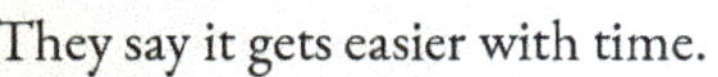

They say it gets easier with time.

Or does time just press more against your heaving chest—
causing you to choke on each laboured breath;
creating glimpses of altered realities that fade in and out of view—
barely tangible?

Yet, I can still smell the tones of your perfume
and hear your stories ringing through my weeping ears.

Maybe if I can just make it through this heavy-laden fog
I can find my way back to your warm embrace—
one final time to say the proper goodbye
that is still wrapped within the confines of my soul;
to tell you that I am sorry
for all those years you were in pain, that I couldn't ease.

To tell you that even though
we fought like fire and ice,
I still love you more than this heart can hold.
Maybe then I can finally lay down this battered sword
I've been carrying for so very long,
and find my peace among the living.

Sara Jama

Screaming into the void—
unheard cries rattle back like rusty chains
being run across long-forgotten prison bars.
Just mere mirages lost to ever-biding time;
fading into the fog—my presence has been
a fading whisper in the wind.

Can you really see me?
See the endless words bleeding from my pen?
Hear the desperation of my pleas—
spilling from parched lips?
If I reach out and touch you,
will these fingers freeze under your cruelty?
Can you show me some much-needed sympathy?

Under the harsh night of another bleak winter,
my brittle heart is shattering in your suffocating hands—
and I can't sense spring approaching this endless torment,
nor feel the warmth of the sun pouring
over the unreachable horizon.

*Only the irreversible descent of love
are locked within the confines of this
fading reality.*

Screaming

Love is Pain

Rays of moonlight gleam through abandoned branches.
Frosted blades of grass crackle under the weight of a heavy heart.
A lost soul desperately searches every corner of the globe
for a love that will never return.

Praying that the angels hear her weeping and show some mercy.
Years of loneliness weigh heavily on sloping shoulders
and aching bones.

Her lover's ghost fades in and out of view, slipping through the
shadows—playing tricks with an already fragile psyche.

Memories becoming distorted, did she ever *truly* exist?
Fragmented echoes of her voice reverberate in the bitter night—
snapping everything back to reality.

Just keep moving—as the blood from cracked feet
seeps through what is reminiscent of disintegrating leather soles
The smell of ferrous iron mixes with sour tears, creating arid acid
—gradually eroding sorrowful lips—
dripping down the larynx, silencing the vocal chords.

Her soul is being eaten inside-out by a lost love—and that pain
will haunt her until the realm of time ceases to exist.

As the sun kisses the burnt-umber horizon,
the torture will end for but a mere moment—
just until the moon glistens o'er the cliff
where her lover took her life,
resetting a frantic search forevermore.

Sara Jama

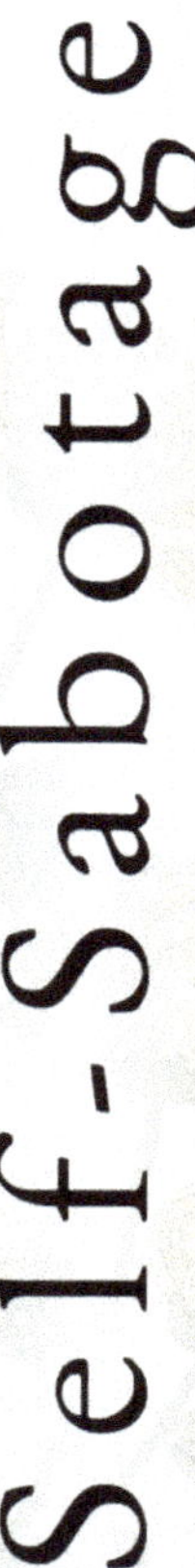

Translucent raindrops hit splintering wood,
freezing into the veins of this crumbling structure;
Expanding and contracting with each dreary season.
Dying grass dots the snow laden landscape,
encompassing a harsh emptiness.

Screeching winds whip, breaking an incessant silence;
startling me awake from a restless slumber—filled with
harsh nightmares and queasy recollections
of a time when I could reach out and touch
your delicate skin, kiss your silken lips, smell the hints
of floral shampoo drifting through the air...
before self-sabotage ate ever so gingerly
at my racing thoughts; slowly burrowing into my
polluted bloodstream - infecting my heart—
decaying it piece by piece until all I saw
was manufactured guilt behind every "stolen" glance.

I Read lies into the words that used to be reassurance.
Paranoia snipped at my unravelling nerves,
pushing you further from the warmth
that once filled our loving home,
furthermore cementing my self-fulling prophecy;

"Forever alone until the ravenous crows
come to pick at my unsettled bones."

Love is Pain

Foggy windows rattle
the bare bones of this vacant house.
Ghosts of you fade away into the empty shadows.
Echoes of your voice still reverberate off the steel beams.
Tears ricochet off of warping walnut floorboards.
Even my body is becoming a shell of what it once was.
**One heartbeat, a shallow breath away
from crossing through the veils.**

An endless winter blows in from the impending horizon.
Pristine, ivory snow slips in between the cracks of the
crumbling ceiling, dusting the strands of my auburn hair—
minuscule reminders that even Demeter
weeps for Persephone.

Grief weighs heavy throughout this moonless night;
I feel a bleak loneliness as vast as the Mariana Trench.
Dropping to the heartless floor, lying in the fetal position,
I silently scream into the void, hoping
the angels will hear my pleas.
Yet my fate has been sealed with this bitter poison,
clinging to memories
that become more distant as each second ticks.
The wick of my candle dimmed slowly from view
as your soul left me that fateful day,
floating into the nether—out of my grasp forevermore.

Forevermore

About the Author

Ghada Khalil

Ghada Khalil, hailing from Sudan, was once a little daydreamer. She had big dreams of becoming a writer. But, as we know, life can be all serious and grown-up. So Ghada ended up in the corporate world, feeling like a fish out of water. Deep down, she knew she needed to shake things up. After all, what's life without a little adventure?

Then one day, a bolt of inspiration hit Ghada. Why not sit down and write her very first novel? The spark of inspiration has been lit ever since, and Ghada now spends most of her time penning poetry and prose.

Find her on Instagram @brushandpentales

Letters to No One

You Had Me At Goodbye

Corridor of Conscience

Haunting Hymns

Dead, But Still Living

Red Lipstick

The Cold Keeps Coming In

A Quiet Goodbye

Doesn't The Day
Know Grief?

Hibernating Heart

An Apparition Now

Choking on Flowers

Ghada Khalil

*A*s I sit here, surrounded by emptiness, I find myself composing a letter to you within my thoughts. It speaks of how I become lost in the depths of your eyes, losing all bearings; no map nor stars could guide me back. I lose touch with reason and logic, satisfied in my delightful madness, happily adrift and lost in thoughts of you.

If I were to find you, my love for you would run deep, the oceans themselves, envied by the depth of our love. I would pen letters to you each passing day, for even until my last breath, words would fail to capture the enormity of my affection, my deep love for you.

Until that moment arrives, I will continue writing letters to no one, my heart's whispers captured in these unsent words.

GK

Love is Pain

*F*rom the moment your goodbye slipped into the air,
a sudden ache settled within;
a haunting pull of longing
that screamed through the corridors of my heart.

You had me at goodbye;
a paradoxical twist in the tale.
As you turned away, I found myself pulled closer—
a feeling I couldn't quite explain.

Your parting words became a siren's call in my head—
made me want you more than before.
Your departure—a catalyst for a yearning;
a desire born in the wake of your farewell.

With every step you took, a silent plea emerged;
to turn back time, to change the course,
to hold onto that goodbye a little longer—
and to find a way back to you.

♡ G.K

You Had Me at Goodbye

In the crowd
   of an airport's hurried commotion,
I knew our paths would cross.
Among the bustling crowds,
our parallel lives met briefly—
an unexpected encounter.

                              As we walked,
                    our shoulders brushed,
                        our hands grazed,
            and in that fleeting moment,
                    time seemed to bend.

Our eyes met,
locking in a familiar connection,
suspended in a timeless pause.

                The world hushed for a heartbeat—
      a conversation held within that shared gaze.

A breath held,
acknowledging the story between us—
a chapter unfinished.

            But then, as swiftly as it happened,
                reality snapped back into place.

      The airport's pulse resumed, and we parted ways
      carried by separate flights and diverging destinies.

In opposite directions, we hurried on,
carrying on in the corridor of conscience—
in that suspended moment,
forever imprinted in our minds.

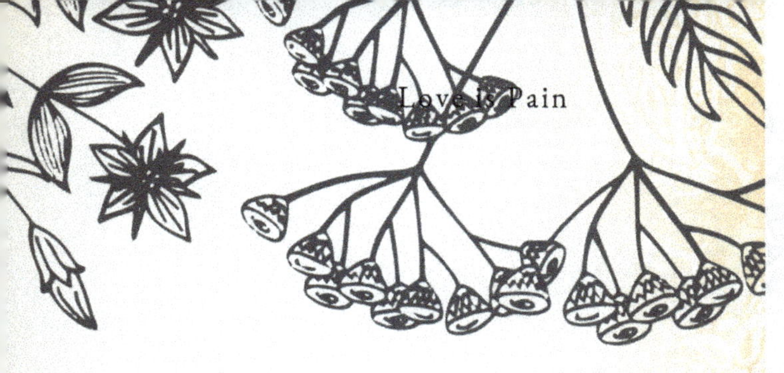

*I*n the midst of her pain, a song plays softly
as he tears her heart, cruelly stamping it astray.
She screams, but the music drowns her cries—
the radio gets louder—a deaf'ning surprise.

"Remember our love," she pleads,
but his eyes—they've turned;
he's become a monster—cruel and haughty.
The song blares louder, drowning her wails—
she shields her ears from the melody that prevails.

Is the song more disturbing than his monstrous act?
A question amongst chaos, a heart that's cracked.
The scars etched on her chest, a permanent sore.
The melody, a haunting hymn, for love is no more.

Her heart's wounds, scars she'll forever wear within.
The song will linger, a reminder of when love grew thin.
A haunting hymn for the day their love turned to dust.
Most of us carry haunting hymns—
of scars and pain that will never mend.

Dead But Still Living

She's there on the bench,
with the task at hand, but feels empty—
just a shell of a person.
No goals, no dreams.
I'm not sure if she's alive—
maybe a ghost, or just in my head.
She barely talks.
Much like a puppet, someone else controls
what she does, eats, and feels.
She constantly tries to shut off her mind,
to numb it, to escape her dull life.
She's alive but feels dead inside—
she's dead but still living.

Red Lipstick

Where should I begin to tell her tale?
She was young, carrying a life within.
With a swollen belly and a heart filled with fear,
she lived each day, shedding silent tears.

Her husband, a tempest of rage
with fists like thunderstorms—
he'd twist her hair and drag her across the room,
leaving her battered on the cold, hard ground.
Many nights, she was left to sleep
on the kitchen's cold, hard floor.

Her delicate face was covered in bruises.
Makeup and red lipstick were her saving grace.
Cuts on her lips—hidden beneath the deep, red lipstick—
hid the pain in her eyes.

Her tears were a silent plea, longing to be freed.
In the shadows, she'd cry,
longing for a love that could calm her fears.
Alone in the silence, she'd shed her tears,
but the scars of abuse lingered until her very end.

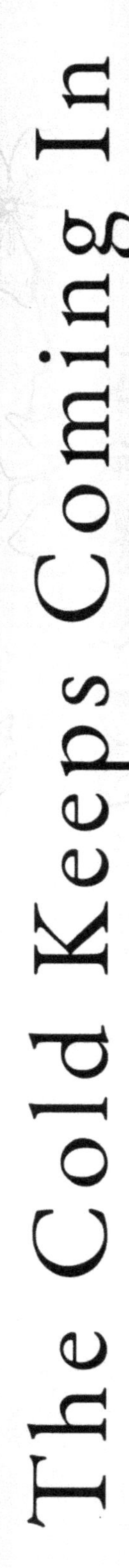

The Cold Keeps Coming In

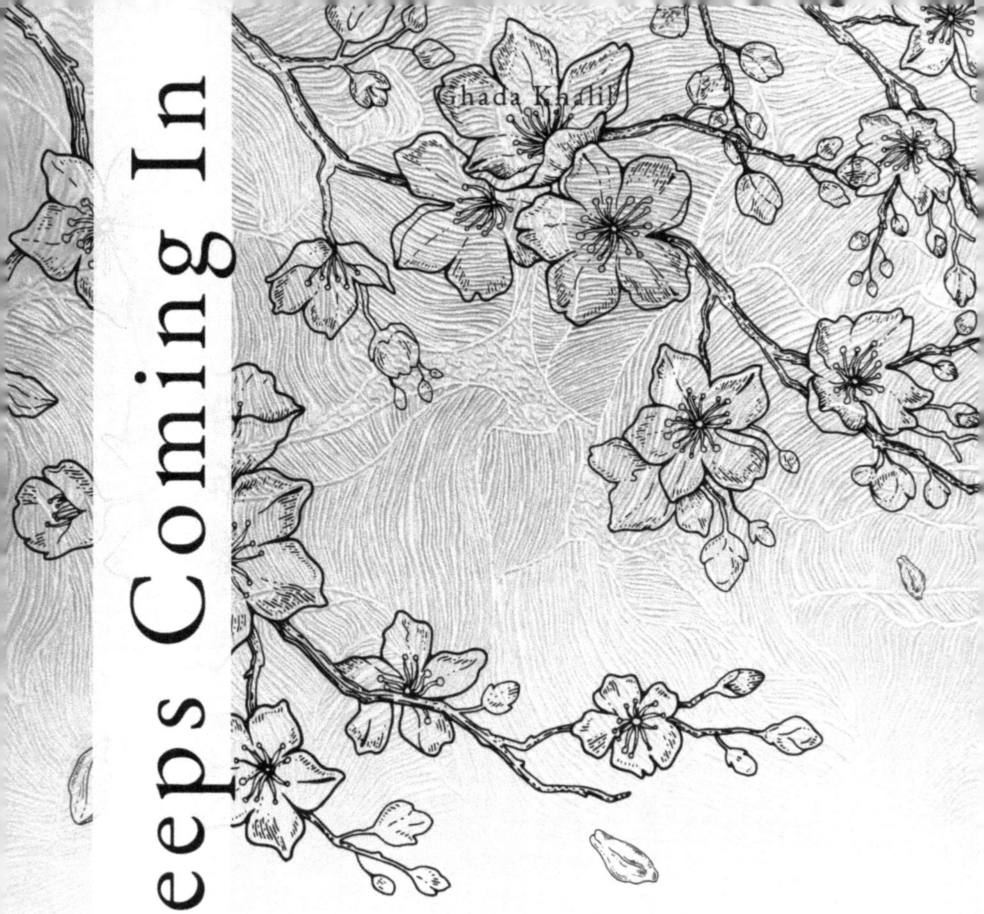

Ghada Khalil

The cold keeps coming in,
slipping through our fragile bond.
A chill lingers, unaddressed,
creeping into moments, a silent intruder.

Sneaking through the cracks,
a persistent guest, that stays—uninvited.
Finding ways past barriers, unblocked,
no matter how tightly shut.

It's in the icy silence that lingers
in the frosty whispers.
The cold keeps coming in,
a rift between hearts quietly spread.

♡GK

A Quiet Goodbye

We laughed and joked, but deep down,
I knew this was the last time—the final farewell.
Every moment, every look I held dear,
knowing it was the end, a goodbye so clear.

Saying good night, a quiet goodbye.
In that moment, I felt it to the core.
Our final farewell—perfectly disguised,
a quiet goodbye, our parting—silently cried.

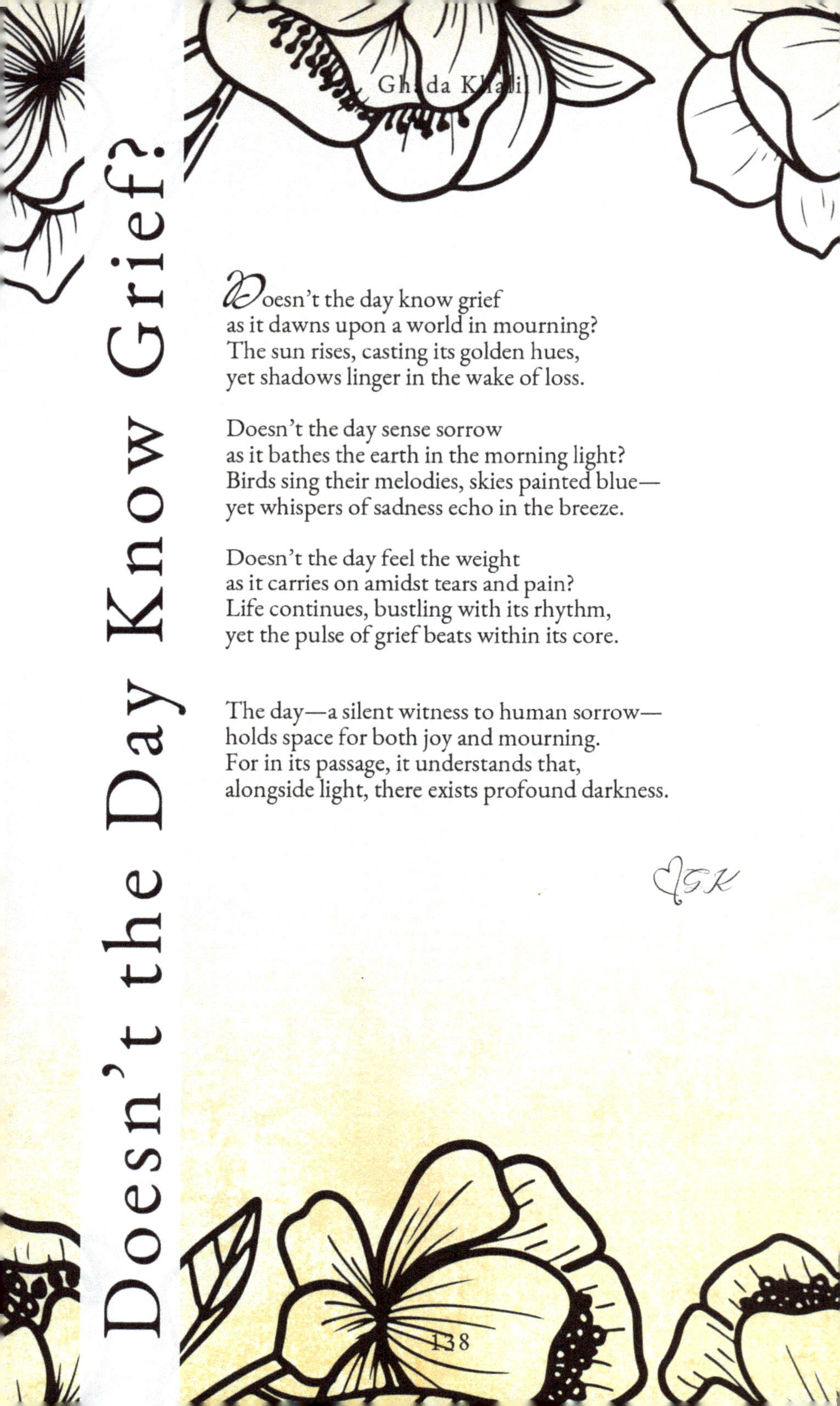

Doesn't the Day Know Grief?

Ghada Khalil

Doesn't the day know grief
as it dawns upon a world in mourning?
The sun rises, casting its golden hues,
yet shadows linger in the wake of loss.

Doesn't the day sense sorrow
as it bathes the earth in the morning light?
Birds sing their melodies, skies painted blue—
yet whispers of sadness echo in the breeze.

Doesn't the day feel the weight
as it carries on amidst tears and pain?
Life continues, bustling with its rhythm,
yet the pulse of grief beats within its core.

The day—a silent witness to human sorrow—
holds space for both joy and mourning.
For in its passage, it understands that,
alongside light, there exists profound darkness.

G.K

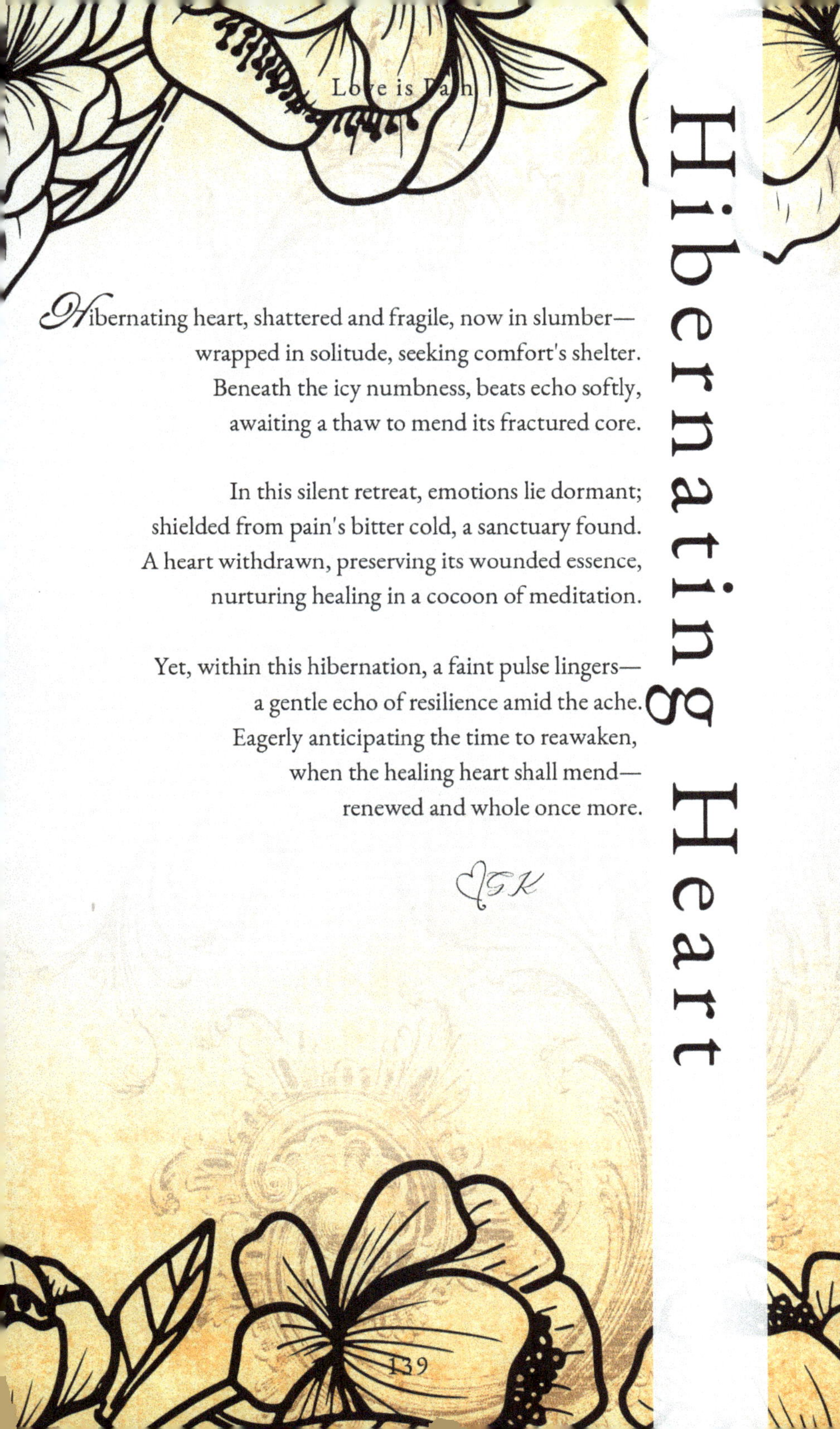

Hibernating Heart

Hibernating heart, shattered and fragile, now in slumber—
wrapped in solitude, seeking comfort's shelter.
Beneath the icy numbness, beats echo softly,
awaiting a thaw to mend its fractured core.

In this silent retreat, emotions lie dormant;
shielded from pain's bitter cold, a sanctuary found.
A heart withdrawn, preserving its wounded essence,
nurturing healing in a cocoon of meditation.

Yet, within this hibernation, a faint pulse lingers—
a gentle echo of resilience amid the ache.
Eagerly anticipating the time to reawaken,
when the healing heart shall mend—
renewed and whole once more.

♡SK

Ghada Khalil

An Apparition Now

In the hospital room, a loved one's fading breath—
life slipping away in silent surrender.
A soul departing, crossing the ethereal divide,
transitioning from present to spectral apparition.

As the heart's beat wanes, a departure is felt.
The worldly tether snaps and yet, lingers near.
A departure—witnessed, a transition unseen;
from mortal form to an otherworldly presence.

The hospital's sterile walls now hold memories,
echoes of laughter, conversations now—still.
An apparition arises, transcending the final moments—
a dear one's essence transformed—a ghostly silhouette.

No longer confined by the bounds of flesh,
a spectral presence wanders; a familiar spirit—
whispers in the corridors, a comfort unseen.
An apparition now in the echoes of the hospital's halls.

Let me breathe you in, your sweet-scented flowers,
an intoxicating bouquet of memories and longing.

Allow me to immerse myself in your presence,
lavender-scented salts, a baptism in your being.
Let me bathe in you, in the sounds of your fragrance,
a cleansing ritual in the essence of your soul.

And when our communion is done,
leave me among your lingering blooms.
Choking on flowers, the remnants of your existence—
even as I gasp, I am surrounded by your essence.

As I struggle, breaths hitching in my chest,
each gasp longing for your tender touch.
Dying, yet enveloped in your lingering perfume,
I find peace in this fragrant farewell, drowning in you.

♡GK

Choking on Flowers

About the Author

Maria Thérèse Williams

Maria Thérèse Williams has lived her whole life in the county of Kent, England. She is the author of the Roaming Reflections collections, all available on Amazon. She loves creative expression, being as comfortable with physical choreography as literary choreography.

She is married with three grown-up children—and her family is her greatest treasure. A close second was her community dance school, which she created and ran for 12 years until retiring in 2016.

As well as her 30 years as a teacher of dance, Maria has garnered a wide range of other professional experiences, including human resources across banking and retail and support working in the NHS for departments such as learning disabilities, dementia support, and cancer services.

Her poetry and prose feature in anthologies such as *Absolutely Poetry*, produced by Wheelsong Books, and *Shadows of the Past are Wings of Future*. She has been featured in *Open Door Magazine* and can often be heard on BBC Radio Kent's Upload program. Her work *"Nurture Nature"* features throughout the documentary film "When the Rare Orchid Blooms" by Film Café Co-op.

She loves all art but, ultimately, loves to read, write, and dance. Her muse is life itself, inspired by psychology, spirituality, nature, relationships, and all the many aspects of existence in this universe.

You can find her poetry and prose at:
Instagram at https://Instagram.com/@roaming_reflections
Facebook Page: www.facebook.com/RoamingReflections
or hear some of them at her
YouTube channel at Roaming Reflections: YouTube

Sticks & Stones
Memory of Me
Conjoining Souls
The Changed Path
Let Me Go
Manpower
Lasting Spell
Slain
Piercing Percipience
Cruel Scrawl
Hearts Misguided
Harrow Shadow
Rainbow Cradle
Maria Thérèse Williams

Maria Thérèse Williams

Sticks & Stones
(Sticks and Stones may Break our Bones but Words and Actions Linger)

We suffer

Writhe, freeze, unravel, lash out
Our very selves threatened
It's instinctive to react
Physical, psychological, emotional
counteractions
Because we're miraculously designed
With a sense of self-protection

Pain strikes

By hammer, heat, hate or loss
We feel the very moment
Harm calls to threaten us
Our perception, understanding
Set the wheels of motion turning
Complex and enduring
Or swift and simple curse

Love hurts

Conditioned assumptions of romance
Hide the existential truth
To give yourself to others
Can be an everlasting noose
The joy it brings is only seen
The moment it is lost

Sweet memory

Sensations of the soul
Recollect who we connect to
The ones who make us whole
Succumb or survive?
The price to feel alive
Quality of feeling
The power behind our drive

And the secret to survival?
To yourself give time, be kind.

JMTW

Maria Thérèse Williams

May the flow of your memories run gently,
The calm of my absence bring tranquility
Comfort reign in my more peaceful energy
My silence give you space to see the good in me.

May I still cause laughter with my silliness
For all who walk this earth leave a mess
May my errs bring you lessons that you treasure
Echoes of my quirks bring some pleasure.

Forgive all the chaos that I may have caused
Recall any little happiness I hope I brought
Know that my love for you will always be
Let my efforts settle gently in your memory.

MTW

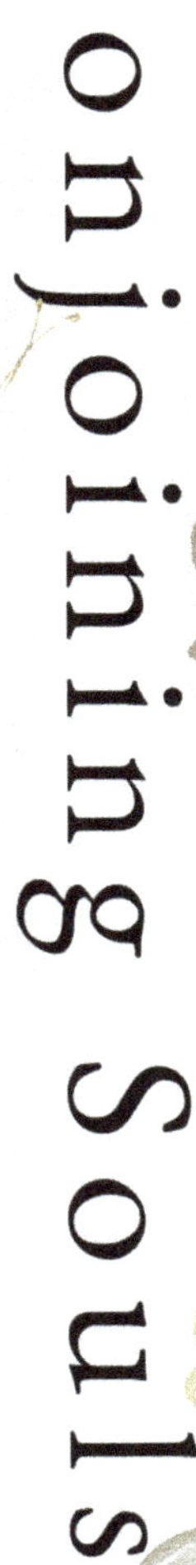

Two separate entities
Promising togetherness forever and a day
No matter if their time remaining here
Is decades or a day
Looking into each other's eyes
Before other eyes and souls to witness
That even when time on earth is brief
We trust in eternal oneness
Hope
Love
Transcends prognoses
There's not a dry eye in the house
Declaring your freedom to choose each other
Contracting to act as one forever
Across the realms
In your own, beautiful world
Weaving your essence into a singular stream
With your surrounding loved ones willing you well
Their smiles beam as their eyes and hearts swell
Tears of joy flow freely
For your conjoining souls to sail
In safety to your heart's desired dream
Love deeply
Time is a mere illusion of humanity
Your essences now sail as one through eternity
This moment is wondrous
Humbled, I creep away, silently pray
You have both drawn strength from your special day

<h3>Maria Thérèse Williams</h3>

The Changed Path

My footing is precarious on this unfamiliar path
My progress obscured by wisps of new fog
My mood is weighted by the engulfing shadows
And I miss having you as my guide

The trees line my way like guards of my grief
Their roots interrupt the fall of my feet
This trail feels so lonely when it was once our home
And I miss having you by my side

Birdsong, at times, breaks this baffling silence
The sun occasionally breaks through the trees
Curious creatures approach me sometimes
And it feels like this sadness could slide

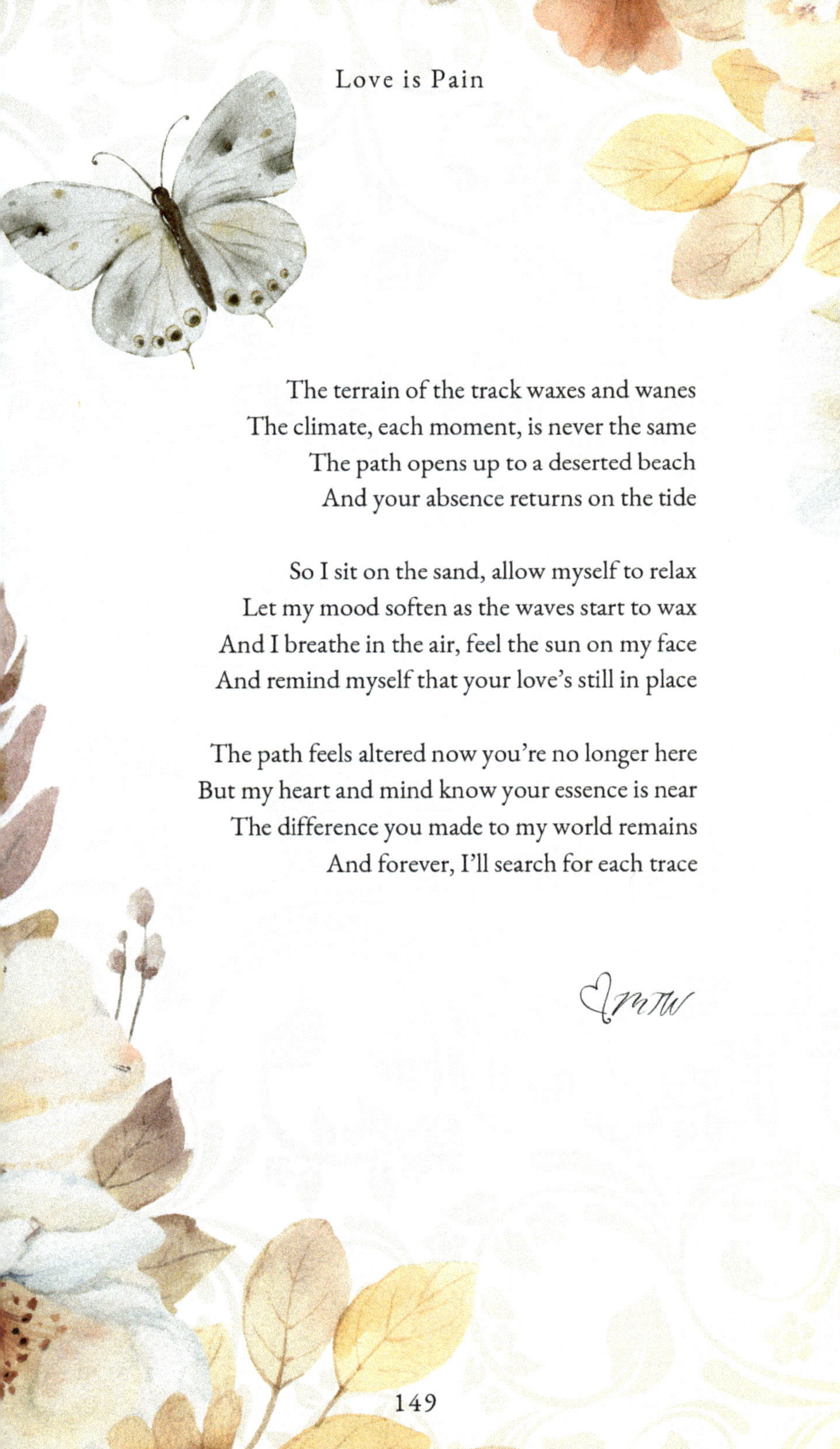

Love is Pain

The terrain of the track waxes and wanes
The climate, each moment, is never the same
The path opens up to a deserted beach
And your absence returns on the tide

So I sit on the sand, allow myself to relax
Let my mood soften as the waves start to wax
And I breathe in the air, feel the sun on my face
And remind myself that your love's still in place

The path feels altered now you're no longer here
But my heart and mind know your essence is near
The difference you made to my world remains
And forever, I'll search for each trace

Maria Thérèse Williams

Can you feel me looking on
Watching while you feel like weeping?
Do you feel you must go on
Whilst thinking of me always sleeping?
My energy, my very essence
I believe you know it well
So how am I to cease existing
When still in stories that you tell?
How can I not still be with you
When love for me is all around?
Look beyond the earthly walls
And hear me in familiar sounds
Gradually, you'll let me go
Release my spirit to fly freely
But in moments that your feeling low
A strength will reach you, sent from me

MTW

Let Me Go

Man Power

A tough exterior, learned lies
He hid the hurt behind his eyes
He longed to tell of his dedication
Instead, his fists flew in frustration
He's mad, he's bad, not worth a jot
Deserved of every cold rejection
Love's the fault; makes real men weak
Learned historic subjugation

Lasting Spell

*K*nowing you were magical
And now you're with the stars
Life seems a little empty now
But memories warm my heart
You cast a spell upon me
I was blessed to be your friend
I am better for knowing you
And that love will never end

Maria Thérèse Williams

Slain

She lay, slain
Her heart in pieces
The cause, the blame
Simple loneliness

♡MTW

*Y*ears bring wisdom as experience grows
They claim friendship in their tread
Wisdom does naivety expose
And romance drops down, dead
But love is not a flowery thing;
A delicate situation
Love has strength, endures all things
That's the power of creation
Pain is one side of the sword
Whilst our dreams shine on the other
But the piercing punctures the very thing
We hold tight to with our lover

MTW

Piercing Percipience

Maria Thérèse Williams

Cruel Scrawl

Stains of pain run with my ink
Cursive claims of passion
Leaving shadows on the page
Injecting scrawls of tension
Calligraphic correspondence
Of a need kept at a depth
For love embraces everything
And hasn't broken yet
I write of dreams I can't quite catch
A reality obscured
Rhymes of reason dissipate
I've learned to hate what I adored

Hearts Misguided

*Y*our embrace burns where it used to heal
Your words cut deep and sharp
Your presence pricks at my every pore
Your absence is a balm
Our hearts know only a single space
We've shared so many years
But every murmur of romance
Has condensed into our tears

Harrow Shadow

*I*t stands in the shadows, watching
Ever waiting, never ceasing to count
Every single moment spent on doubting
It counts my worries, one by one
I persevere
It knows I know it's here
But I love any way.

Maria Thérèse Williams

Rainbow Cradle

You may not see me grow up tall
But I can touch the sky,
You may not hear my laughter
But know I have no cause to cry.
I already know a billion things-
No need to go to school,
Others learn of far-off lands
But I can roam them all.

All the dreams you had for me
The hopes that you had built,
May make grief feel like anger
Or unnecessary guilt.
But there was nothing you could do;
Fate held my destiny,
This world is simply too constrained
For my boundless energy.

Love is Pain

I thank you all for wanting me
And investing so much love,
I'll be your precious memory
When times may feel too tough.
Wrap your arms around each other
Don't be afraid to speak my name,
My presence may be ethereal
But I love you just the same.
The fabric of my Angel wings
Is a weave of all your care
And if you feel a gentle breeze
Imagine I am there.
Taking time out from my play
To embrace the thoughts you send me.
Sharing colour from my rainbow world
With my loving family.

MTW

About the Author

Reena Doss

Writing is Reena Doss' first voice of expression, followed closely by art and creativity. Through the encouraging platform provided by the Instagram community she reclaimed her lost voices, evolved a few others, and discovered new ones along the way. Born in Calcutta with roots drawn from Chennai and Pondicherry, Reena Doss has lived most of her life in the south of India—Bangalore. You can try and catch her but it may not always be possible as she is generally off on adventures: flying on phoenix wings, swimming into the deep with mermaids, and chasing fiery dragons down for stories. Visit her website to learn more. www.reenadoss.com

Reena Doss

I felt alone
in the way the island does
despite the ocean wrapping itself around it
loving its curves and rough borders...
Funny how you can envy an island
and long for even a lake or pond or puddle
to hold you through the nightmarish nights
than the dry desolate waste
that surrounds your heart,
while rocks and stones
scrape its edges
making *you*
bleed.

-The hope of an island

Breadcrumbs

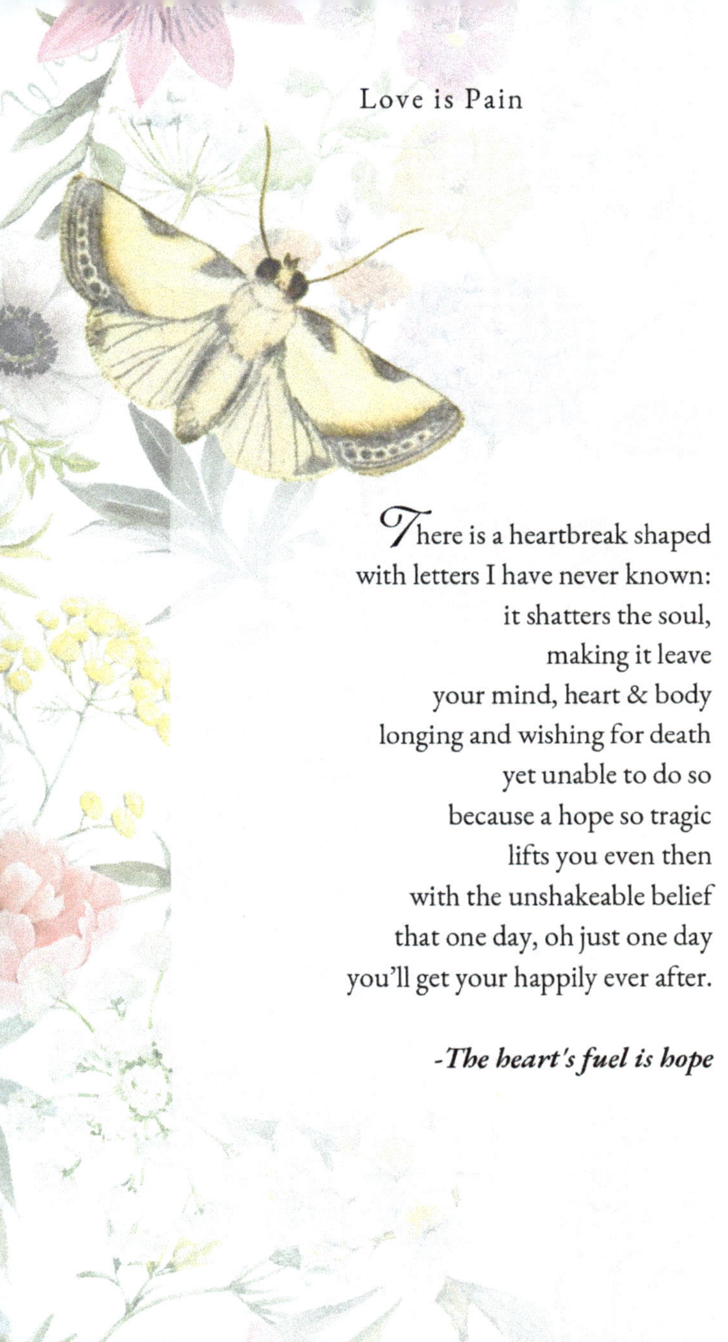

Shattered

*T*here is a heartbreak shaped
with letters I have never known:
it shatters the soul,
making it leave
your mind, heart & body
longing and wishing for death
yet unable to do so
because a hope so tragic
lifts you even then
with the unshakeable belief
that one day, oh just one day
you'll get your happily ever after.

-The heart's fuel is hope

The Third One

Reena Doss

If she had known any better...
but how could she?
He treated her so prettily in the beginning.
She was a green girl who couldn't have
held up defenses even if she'd tried.
He easily picked out her giving heart
without having to win it.
She gave it to him on a platter
because she was never one to play games.
She watched him turn it around in fascination,
her happiness bubbling over thinking he saw her
when all he saw was a solution to his loneliness.
When he twisted it, she gasped
not able to understand why, oh why,
was he slyly watching her flinch
when he trod over boundaries
she did not know she had?
He pricked the veins of her beating heart
like a child with an interesting toy,
wondering how he could dissect it
and put it back together to make it his,
not valuing its open joy as it looked at him
in complete love and trust believing
his words when she shouldn't have.

Her first love was simple, complex, and yet easy to forget.
But wasn't *he*... supposed to be the love of her life?
She'd forgotten about reading how those second loves
were supposed to be the most painful kind.
She didn't understand the rules of his game
as he left her alone in multiple mazes after dark,
knowing she didn't know the way out of there,
then swooping in to rescue her
when she began to fear she was losing her mind.
And she would be so thankful,
forgetting that it was him who placed her here.
This cruel back and forth ran its course
as she began to question him.

-The third one was worth the wait

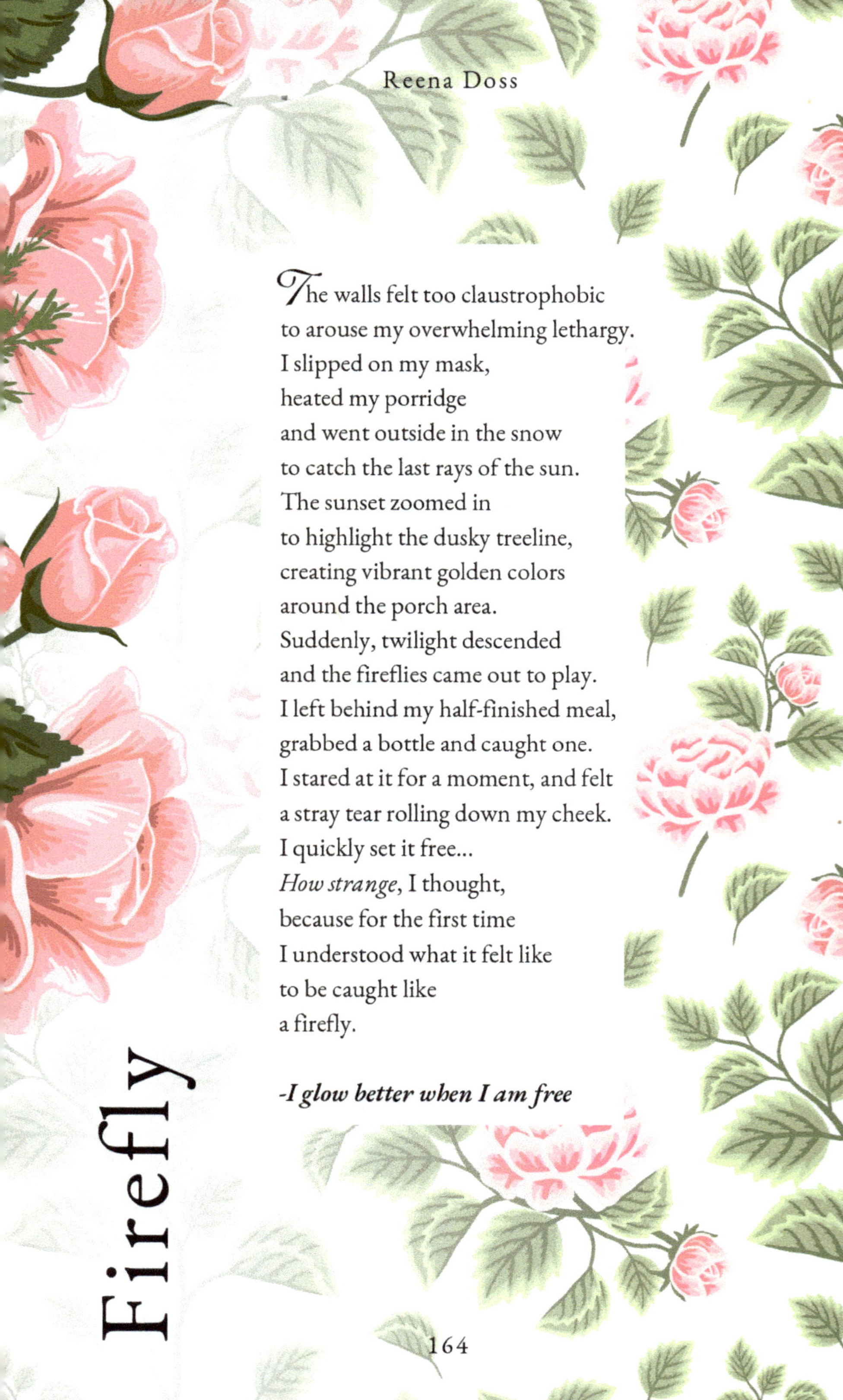

Reena Doss

The walls felt too claustrophobic
to arouse my overwhelming lethargy.
I slipped on my mask,
heated my porridge
and went outside in the snow
to catch the last rays of the sun.
The sunset zoomed in
to highlight the dusky treeline,
creating vibrant golden colors
around the porch area.
Suddenly, twilight descended
and the fireflies came out to play.
I left behind my half-finished meal,
grabbed a bottle and caught one.
I stared at it for a moment, and felt
a stray tear rolling down my cheek.
I quickly set it free...
How strange, I thought,
because for the first time
I understood what it felt like
to be caught like
a firefly.

-I glow better when I am free

Firefly

Walk In Faith

*L*oving you was not wrong
because it taught me how to love gloriously
and if I could love someone
who did not love me
in the way it might have been,
I cannot imagine
how I would love the one
the Sun brings
for when you are
able to grasp things clearly
from other perspectives,
you can see rainbows aplenty,
when otherwise—
you'd have just noticed
an empty sky.

-Dismiss your own understanding of events

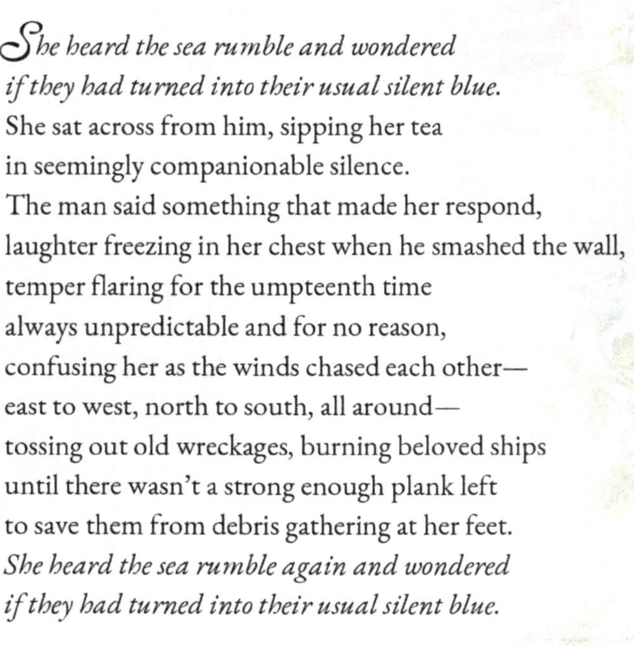

She heard the sea rumble and wondered
if they had turned into their usual silent blue.
She sat across from him, sipping her tea
in seemingly companionable silence.
The man said something that made her respond,
laughter freezing in her chest when he smashed the wall,
temper flaring for the umpteenth time
always unpredictable and for no reason,
confusing her as the winds chased each other—
east to west, north to south, all around—
tossing out old wreckages, burning beloved ships
until there wasn't a strong enough plank left
to save them from debris gathering at her feet.
She heard the sea rumble again and wondered
if they had turned into their usual silent blue.

-Silent waters carry the deepest sorrows

Trigger

I let you go,
thinking I had pulled the trigger on myself
but I was surprised to find
that the only thing that splintered
was the glass idea of you
out of my head.
Broken and outside of me,
I realized that you didn't belong
to my shaping.

-*You never built roots in my heart*

Withheld

*T*ied up in compliments,
bitter nuggets of sarcasm
slithered like a narrow stream
from a spring,
reluctant to flow
out of a beloved
mountain.

-*Why did you grudge me kindness?*

About the Author

Kalpesh Desai

Kalpesh Desai is a successful tech serial entrepreneur who has used poetry as a medium to process his thoughts, breakthroughs, and distinctions. Kalpesh is a management graduate from India's foremost business school. He has over 30 years of experience in creating and running successful technology firms servicing financial services, insurance, manufacturing, retail, distribution, and oil & gas sectors.

Kalpesh has also been recognized as one of the Top 10 Financial Technology CEOs in 2020 by CEO Insight and has been featured in Insead's case study of 3i Infotech where his go-to-market strategy that led to 3i Infotech's organic growth was highlighted.

He is currently the President and CEO of Agile Financial Technologies, in addition to serving as a mentor on the advisory and operating boards of other large enterprises.

Kalpesh has recently released his debut poetry book, *Jasmines In Her Hair,* available on Amazon.

Scan the QR Code on the right, to view his website and find the various social media platforms he frequents.

Where Does Sorrow Go?
Unfulfilled
Haunted
Grief
Just in Case You Wanted to Know
Is Happiness a Myth?
Missing
Cheating on You
Let's Rewrite the Rules
You Are Not Here
Kalpesh Desai

Kalpesh Desai

$\mathcal{W}$here does sorrow go,
when our eyes are dry, and we feel no more?

Where do we bury love,
when all we see are dark clouds above?

Where do our shame and disgrace hide,
with whom do they now confide?

They beckon our sanity, lurking in the shadows,
of what we thought were once our mighty boughs.

Whispering ghosts weep under the willows,
teardrops falling over stories, that each falling leaf knows.

And now and again, they grace our memories,
With soft voices carried over the evening breeze.

These ghosts of our past, that are buried deep,
Soaking in the tears that our willows weep.

Aren't the leaves that fall from the same tree, that heal?
Perhaps, we bury those ghosts when our wounds we seal.

Love is Pain

Unfulfilled

I will not rely upon
sorrowful sails cast upon
mournful seas,
nor on fractured hopes
and their tempestuous unease.

I will not let,
unfulfilled expectations and dreams,
lay on a bed of regrets,
slowly tearing at my seams.

I will not let shut doors,
stop me from breaking through those walls,
nor let storms hamper me from reaching those shores,
where they shall hear my voice echoing in their halls.

No tempest shall contain me,
I will bend but I will not break,
I will tuck away every bad memory,
every regret, every heartache.

For I am the captain, and I won't let chaos reign,
When it is time to bring the ship to the shore,
I will learn the terrain.
I will do it now. I have done it before.

And when your memories
come to haunt me again,
when the echoes
of our stories
bring on the pain,
when my anger breaches
the threshold of refrain,
I seek sweeter shores
devoid of disdain,
I seek a home,
where my heart can reign.

♡ KD

Haunted

Grief

Is it possible that we grieve
because we are yet to forgive?
Because their absence hurts more
than their presence ever did before?
Because we cannot take back what we said,
or tell them what remains unsaid?
Because they left without warning, or too soon,
and now we whisper our goodbyes to the moon?
Because there were journeys to complete,
and we couldn't make time to meet?
Because there were promises to keep,
and now all we can do is weep?
Is it possible that grief
is anger, turning over a new leaf?
Is it possible that we grieve
because we are yet to forgive?

Kalpesh Desai

In Case You Wanted to Know

If the rain serenades the song of my tears,
would you not want to know
that the song was about you?

If the howling wind reflects my inner fears,
would you not want to know
that what I most feared was losing you?

When flashes of lightning
bring on old memories—
just know that the thunder that follows
are my cries to you.

When I am soaked to the skin,
I recall our stories,
and how you loved the fresh smell of earth,
and the morning dew.

And, as I watch each raindrop fall,
I remember
how they once lingered on your lips.
I remember
how we would heed their call,
when you shivered
at the touch of my fingertips.

It is this wretched rain
that sings our song—
of a foregone home
to which we used to belong.

And our soul seeks
that which we do not have.
We taint our skies
with golden streaks,
just to see our dreams
cut down in half.
And just when we begin to believe
that happiness is a myth,
there comes the light,
and beckons the dark to leave.
Showing you,
that you were all
that you needed to begin with.

KD

Is Happiness a Myth?

Missing

$\mathcal{I}$ do not know
what guides my lackluster soul,
Is it home?
And all that the heart is missing?
A piece of me endlessly searches to be whole,
paving a path, through a lifetime of trying.
And though I listen to what they tell me,
to manifest all the things that I can be,
it is only the fire that inside me grows,
that makes me unstoppable -
whether the dam dries, or the river flows.

♡ KD

Can love be this intense,
that it does not make any sense?
When I feel like I have cheated on you,
by falling in love with myself anew?
And even this possibility,
could not exist outside of the tranquility
of the space that exists
between me, and you.

Cheating on You

Kalpesh Desai

Let's rewrite the rules tonight,
of this game we play.
Let us not be polite,
when our thoughts are in disarray.
Let the unspoken intensity
break through the labyrinth of desire.
I do not seek serenity
when I want you to light the fire.
And every night,
we become undone.
Let us set our sights
on moments when
we were one.

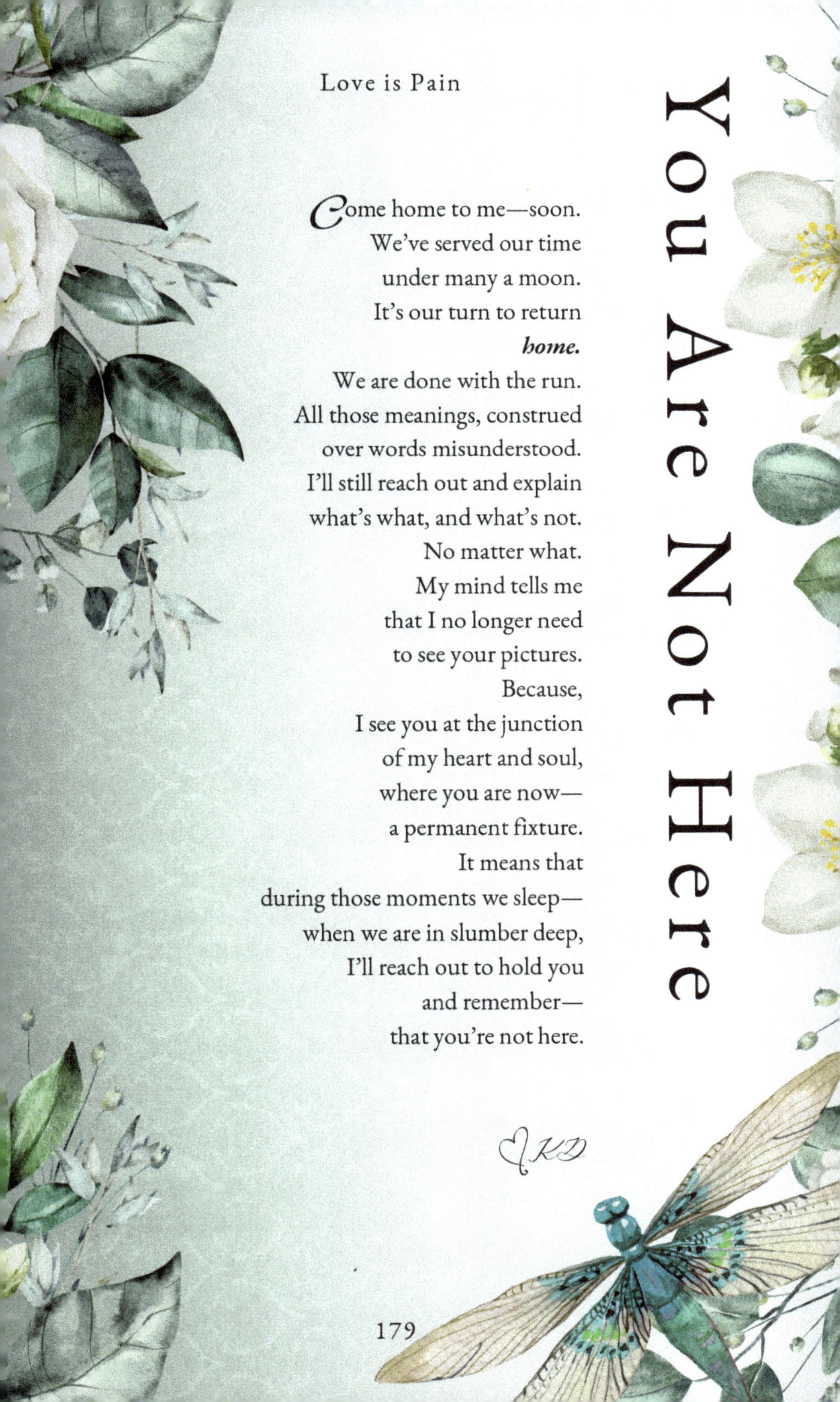

Love is Pain

*C*ome home to me—soon.
We've served our time
under many a moon.
It's our turn to return
home.
We are done with the run.
All those meanings, construed
over words misunderstood.
I'll still reach out and explain
what's what, and what's not.
No matter what.
My mind tells me
that I no longer need
to see your pictures.
Because,
I see you at the junction
of my heart and soul,
where you are now—
a permanent fixture.
It means that
during those moments we sleep—
when we are in slumber deep,
I'll reach out to hold you
and remember—
that you're not here.

179

About the Author

Michael J. Dennis

Michael is a poet and author, his first published collection of poetry, *Sonnets of Love and Life,* expresses his love of the English Sonnet.

Other poetry books: *Ferris Wheels and Candy Floss, Blocks of Stone and Dark Steps, The Colours of My Rainbow,* and *Sonnets of Love and Life 2.*

His first Novel in the *Chronicle of Achren* series *'Thanatus'* introduced Almund Penny to the world followed by three Novellas *'Drugar' 'Werwulf'* and *'Ankou'.*

A massive history fan, he brings much historical detail to even these fantasy books (although many liberties were taken) One of the principal factors found within his poetry and writing is his love of Kent, his home county, and the exploration of historical events and places.

He loves historical fiction by Conn Iggulden, M.C. Scott, Henry Sidebottom, Madeline Miller, Berwick Coates, and Bernard Cornwell.

Reading many of these books far more times than can be seen as healthy, along with many other great storytellers and poets from Keats to Wordsworth, Shakespeare to Wilfred Owen, Vita Sackville West to Sylvia Plath.

Michael, a Man of Kent, husband, father, and grandfather often found a camera in hand wandering the downs, ancient sites, or by the seashore.

On Instagram @mikejdennis5

Pretend

Words Once Said

Balloons

No Bells Tolled

Somewhere Near

Shadows

My Masochist Heart

The Robin

Full Moon O'er the Yew

Under the Stars

Michael J. Dennis

Michael J. Dennis

That I may pretend
as the night descends,
yet my pain ne'er ends—
what price, a smile.

Love lost is my plight.
Will my life take flight;
as the stars burn bright—
yet grey with guile?

Sing sweet love and fear.
Wish that you may hear
whispers in your ear.
You lie alone.

Lady of the Lake;
my lonely heart aches
as I walk this strake.
My fate, now sown.

Pretend

Love is Pain

Words that once said, "For the love of me."
Divine, my heart touched, sacrificed be.
Tender lips brush thee, enraptured lover—
be forever my hypogean plea.
O'er pain! Numb tendrils bind a white hart.
"O heart loves sharp poison dart," spat she.

Love lost in misery, lies glory—
full of skite, as Wolcens doth flurry.
Woven wreaths; a short story 'pon deaths mound,
laid o'er pains wrought whispers, vainglory—
deep sorrow, no absolution—found.
Upon love, crowned my allegory.

A nightingale's melancholy shed
tears o'er a once-rose-petal bed.
What was once said—the loving cup brimming
A bitter reminder: spilt blood is red.
Locked in a mind, no thoughts to be free
This lover's pact of dying—misled.

183

Michael J. Dennis

*Y*ou passed through my dreams of yesteryear
when time once flowed so deep o'er life's weir.
In long-lost hope, a golden sphere—those hours
and April showers, we lost in tears.

Before summer's daisy wreath flowers
slip away; life grows old and dour.
As winter and summer's cowering petals
do scatter and settle o'er the hour.

And that which we hold dear, all seems lost.
Thoughts dwell on the past tonight, embossed
upon my mind's eye to live—tossed again.
These memories remain a thawed frost.

As the wind winds back the year's tonight
I dream and dream; I am young and bright.
To look beyond this misty night of years,
nor write of those fears of endless flight.

For furrowed brow and silvered-white, now—
will prove my dreams false tonight. And how
those summer songs and petalled boughs—too sweet
to last, too sweet to die, yet endow.

At rest, 'pon my lap, pages careworn;
a life-bound, pictures faded and torn.
Shadows greet me, reborn those days gone by.
For a moment, shyly turn to mourn.

Balloons

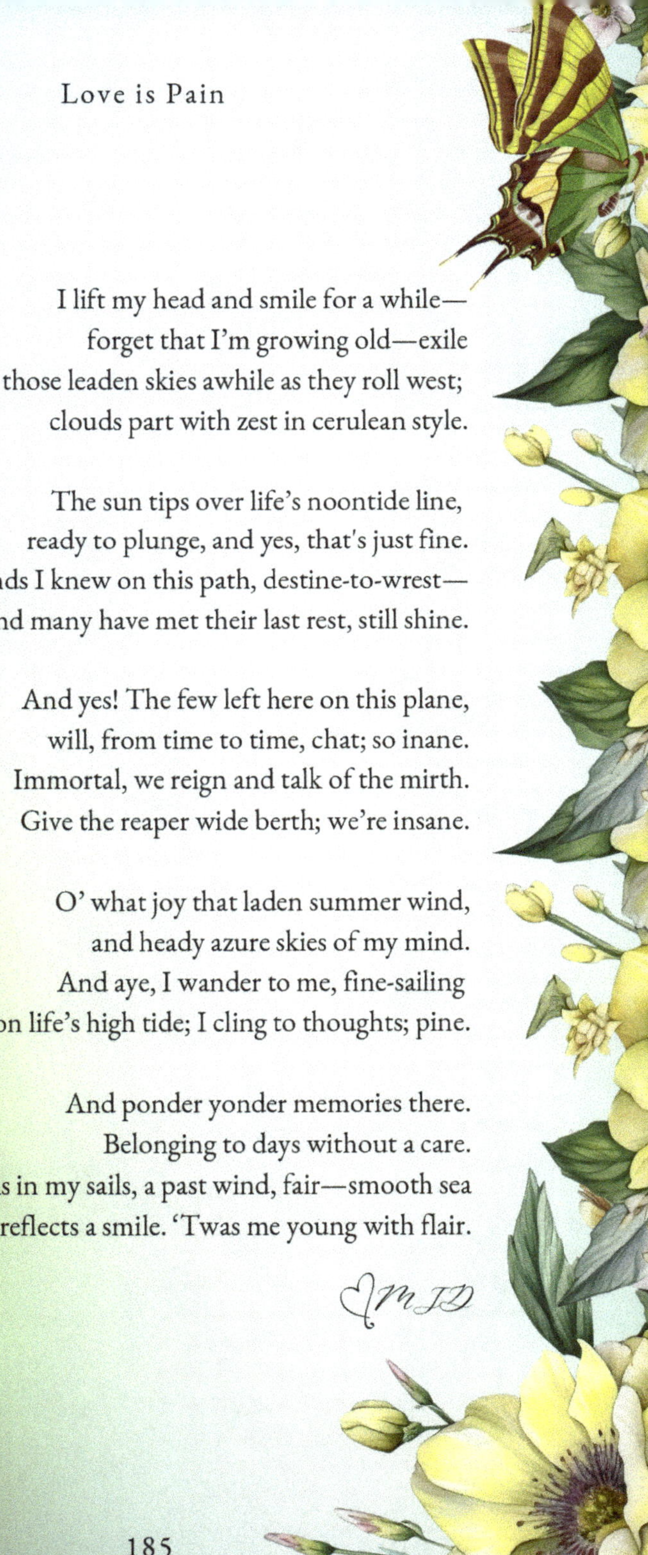

Love is Pain

I lift my head and smile for a while—
forget that I'm growing old—exile
those leaden skies awhile as they roll west;
clouds part with zest in cerulean style.

The sun tips over life's noontide line,
ready to plunge, and yes, that's just fine.
Friends I knew on this path, destine-to-wrest—
and many have met their last rest, still shine.

And yes! The few left here on this plane,
will, from time to time, chat; so inane.
Immortal, we reign and talk of the mirth.
Give the reaper wide berth; we're insane.

O' what joy that laden summer wind,
and heady azure skies of my mind.
And aye, I wander to me, fine-sailing
on life's high tide; I cling to thoughts; pine.

And ponder yonder memories there.
Belonging to days without a care.
As in my sails, a past wind, fair—smooth sea
reflects a smile. 'Twas me young with flair.

Michael J. Dennis

I listened, but no bells tolled.
My suffering that cup overflowed.
No respite to heal my world.
All lost in dreams now unfold.

Hidden deep in the past—none could see
the burrowed loneliness within me.
Abandon free will, for I have none.
Beneath this willow, she weeps for love unspun.

As my tears fall for you,
A beauty loved, do I play the beast?
In this tale of infinite dreams that flew
beyond your eyes, thoughts of paradise, released.

Through your smile, my sun rises.
Hope desert's me. For what do I gain?
Wandering alone in this garden of pain,
an enchantment in my truth surmises:
that bitter pill, and what I will lose.

The willow weeps with me
as my tears fall for you.
All I had missed before—
felt in the love, the pain, the hope.
Oh, beautiful one, my hopes soar.
You'll be mine until my last day is done.

My life without you... without you
I cannot pen my poetry's brightest sun.

I'm lost in the depths of Hades.

Michael J. Dennis

Somewhere Near

The water laps gently somewhere near
I oft but wonder, "Have you been here?"
But left as my footsteps, lonely, trace
that you would have never seen this place.

A magical bay, found such as this,
where we two may share a secret kiss.
And coy; as the sun slips yonder clouds,
I should scream my love for you out loud!

An echo 'tis all in silence shroud
will forever hold my love, ne'er bowed.

MJD

Michael J. Dennis

Shadows

If these words find you, my love,
as we, my dove, came this way.
The days lengthen, I assume;
sad shadows loom in dismay.

Also, cast where you doth pause;
contemplate those laws and watch—
the same sky, the sunsets gloom,
nor presume, nor carve a notch.

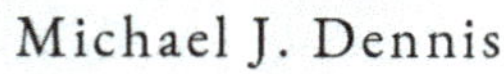

Love is Pain

A day beyond and shiver,
or quiver like fleeting rays.
My wish—to gaze upon you—
it's true, as I think and pause.

Before my failing vision,
as night's incision repeals.
In truth, are we now so wise?
We arise now, in appeal.

Worlds apart, our gods demand—
walk this land, for in my thoughts:
know you better now than then;
love you more, tongue-tied, in knots.

Back then—of forget-me-nots,
they plot; I remember how—
your swift flight from brutish men,
and then, my bright star, my vow.

My fear—we are but playthings
of our gods, and kings, forbid.
Failed you so cruelly, and plead—
as we foolish mortals did.

Michael J. Dennis

My Masochist Heart

Oh! My masochist heart deceives—
leaving me little but to grieve.
My days pass, torn in pain;
tender thoughts of love lodged in my brain.

But you, my love, have taught me well.
Your love placed me under such a wanton spell.
My heart plunged into the deepest freeze
after giving me hope to snatch the keys.

Do you think that after this pain, I can grow?
That I'll ever smile, and the tears no longer flow?
Why do roses bear such brutal thorns?
I'm so punished by love—eternally sworn.

You, my love, took my breath away.
Left bereft, abandoned. Oh! How I pay!
This masochist heart, broken from days gone by;
lonely nights ever racked by my cries.

I'm left locked—trapped within these walls—
whereas no other soul lives to hear my calls.
Come daylight, a smile hides my hurt.
My life has no joy; I've no self-worth.

This trusting heart may someday break free
to find new love and keep my sanity, maybe.
Until that day, my heart grieves for what I've lost;
how you broke my heart—be I, so star-crossed.

Surely I would die if my love for you died first.
My living with this pain—can anything be worse?
That I seek kind release—in death, obtain?
I've sought help, only to be labelled insane.

Please try to understand these caverns of my thoughts
instead of therapy and tying me in knots.
They want me *normal!* Those who've never risked to live!
Why so afraid? Hiding from so much that life can give.

Look into my heart at those gains and losses.
Even on this battlefield, flowers will bloom between the crosses.
So, maybe there's a day when I'll escape.
The broken me fixed—a life once more to take shape.

It is such that friends will ever come and go,
but my masochist heart is mine, just so.

Michael J. Dennis

The Robin

I wander o'er this lonely field;
my solitary footsteps pass.
Cut sheaves of grain e'er wondrous yield;
strums in tune with my thoughts, alas.
A beautiful sound that speaks of pain
in such a melancholic strain—I listen!
O'er the downs profound,
they now overflow with sound.

Of the Robin, her chill-like chant.
A cool mountain pool, at hand,
overflows in a burbling haunt.
A little sad amongst that strand:
so wistful, a voice was ne'er heard.
Throughout the year, emotions stirred,
breaks the silence this autumn morn,
through the misty fingers of dawn.

Love is Pain

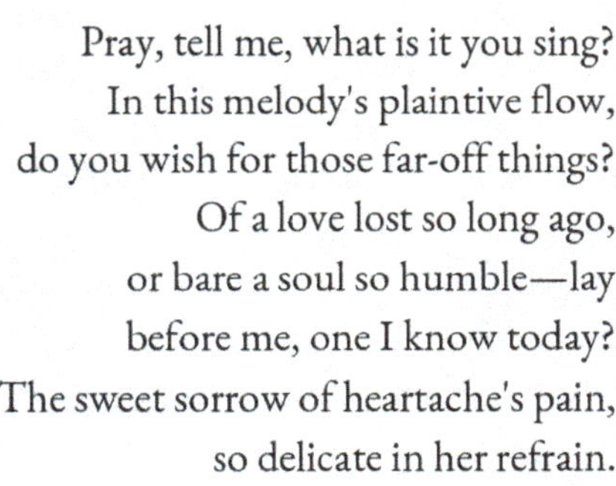

Pray, tell me, what is it you sing?
In this melody's plaintive flow,
do you wish for those far-off things?
Of a love lost so long ago,
or bare a soul so humble—lay
before me, one I know today?
The sweet sorrow of heartache's pain,
so delicate in her refrain.

In what meaning—the Robin sang,
immortal and without ending—
for her singing a painful pang
of those souls, she was attending.
In chilled silence, o'er star-lit sky,
my love lies 'neath the rolling hills,
sweet music 'pon my lips, I bore—
drifts gently 'til I heard no more.

Full Moon O'er The Yew

Michael J. Dennis

Lost in the depths of my mind, a pinprick of light, distant...
I watch the trees; they are black. The light has a silvery hue.
The grass soaks my bare feet as it weeps in tears of grief.
But I am no god. It grips my ankles in supplication,
whispering in soft tones of humility.
A spiritual, vaporous mist inhabits this place,
separated betwixt the worlds of shadowed gravestones.
I simply cannot see where I begin or end.
Long is the way, so hard, that leads from despair up to light.

When the moon has nothing to say,
it looks down, cold, and dispassionate.
White as a corpse, wrapped in its shroud of grief,
it drags at the sea, calling, wishful in its silence—
a stunned expression of complete despair. I live here.
Of faith, the cathedral bells peal a soft rent in the sky.
Ten voices call out, beckoning those who follow...
The mind is in its own place; in itself,
I am lost in the depths of heaven or hell.

The mystic yew tree points to the heavens,
and my eyes lift, following its reach; I find the moon.
She embraces me as a mother, not sweet but stoic.
Misty garments shed, and upon silent wings, the owl sweeps.
As with the years, it's hard to believe in tenderness.
I walk through the doors. Footsteps break the hush.
Carved faces stare as they follow each tortured step.
I kneel, look up—an effigy face softened by flicking candles
looks kindly upon me in particular, with caring eyes.

Have I fallen so far, yet 'twas never my faith?
The clouds are rolling, blossoming forth,
a silvery hush over the watching starlit veil.
Inside the squat cathedral, the saints in their nighttime hue,
floating in ethereal light, watching the distant cold pews.
Their carved features—locked in stiff piety.
My moon knows nothing of this. She is cyclical and free.
And the yew tree, its roots over the millennia touching, reach down.
Speak only of blackness... locked in my thoughts, silent, black, and deep.

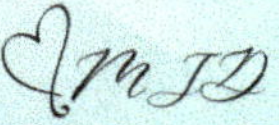

Michael J. Dennis

Under the Stars

*I*f I could ever meet you again,
by the old gate, under the stars,
would I make the same mistakes—
or say those things that should remain unsaid?

Do you think we have changed? So different.
We'd still walk through the lanes,
the bright moon casting her light,
reflecting silver and shining.

So. Perhaps this is a special night.
We would look back, see what we were,
and finally know who we are.
if I could ever meet you again.

Are we so lost? We have strayed so far! Memories
of hurt—still fresh after all these years.
Such sorrow, resting heavily upon our lives,
like the low-rolling dark clouds of a thunderstorm.

You know that I love you still.
If only you would hear my voice.
I cry over the thought of wasted years.
That's how I would feel if you gave me the choice.

Does so much lie empty, happiness closed?
Lost is the lightness of life—the laughter;
all seems touched by winter's cold chill
as I walk the empty avenues of my mind.

Yet through it all, I still see your face,
smiling as on a bright spring day.
You wait for me under the stars.
With your smile the night fades, and our day begins.

You turn upon hearing my voice,
for you love me now, and forever. Yes!
If I could ever meet you again,
I'd tell you all, if given the choice.

About the Author

Miriam Otto

Miriam Otto is a poetess, artist, and a designer who lives in the beautiful German countryside, close to the woods. She loves many things, that is why she is also a photographer, dancer, traveler and learner for life. If she is not traveling or sitting beside the fire and writing, you will find her strolling through the woods behind her house.

But be aware she might cast a spell on you.

She began writing stories and poems ever since she was able to write.

You find her words, art and photos in almost 30 international anthologies and magazines around the world and within her own poetry books, *Wild Fire and Magic, Yellow Drops of Stardust* and, *Who Casts a Spell on Us* with the help of Ink Gladiators Press. And is currently working on her fourth collection for Hedgehog Poetry Press.

Miriam supports artists by giving them a platform through the Voices of Poets community on Instagram and through creative courses she hosts for poets and artists from all over the world. If she is not talking to trees, she will brush up her French and go stay in Paris for two weeks, learn to play piano or take an art history course in Venice.

To connect with Miriam:

Instagram @miriamo77

dreamtravelconnect.com

My First Love

Grow Into Yourself

To My Inner Critic

*Why Isn't There
More Love in The World?*

On To New Adventures

Is This Climate Change?

*When I Listen,
Wonders Happen*

I Love You, I Think

Miriam Otto

Miriam Otto

I still fall in love with words
that play on my tongue.
And the possibility of a lake
in a far away country.
Titicaca—it is the fernweh
that intrigues me.

Once there was a love in my heart,
I call coincidence at seven,
that made me open up for Takkiq
sneezing in Alaska,
while a kangaroo jumps out of a bush
on the other side of the world.

A week later, I stand in front of the class
and recite *a poem*
by heart and found my first love.

Meanwhile,
I fell in love with the simultaneity of snow
at the North Pole
and the summer desert in North Africa.

And animals like the trout
that rhymes with Gazelle in German.

Earth traveled around the sun,
I didn't kiss you before ten.
Just a hushed kiss on your lips
meeting for a second
on our way home. Because I knew
your favorite color.

My First Love

Love is Pain

We never kissed a second time.

But if I hadn't fallen in love with you
at least once
the world would be more silent.

*Note: In dedication to In Dieser Minute
(In this minute) by Eva Rechlin.
A poem, I discovered at an early age.*

Miriam Otto

It is not a dream.
I wish I could have held my breath
a bit longer
as Artemis is running
and pausing at the same time.

She plugs the first signs of spring,
touching some snowdrops with her fingertips
as if their bells create sounds
and moves as if she is a bird
with a green feather dress.

I wish I could have molded deeper
into the fallen leaves
as she turns her head mid-flight.

When are you angry? she asks;
not too loud, not too hushed.
I still lean against my beech,
my knees pressed to my chest
to make me smaller.
I feel the pressure the bark
leaves on me. I am caught
in the rhythm of Artemis questions:

Have you ever growled and screamed so loud
that you awakened the wildest beast within you,
with fangs so strong you could climb up trees?

I wish I said I dreamed of it
until I could leave the ground like you,
until I am so angry I become a stone like you,
until I become water and flow over the land
with my own melody.
I don't answer.

Love is Pain

Artemis knows about my plays
to hide my treasures.

She comes closer, sees my feathers
and looks at my fingers
as if she could see some fur:
My darling, do not worry!
You will be a wildling one day.

And away she is like a deer.

Now, I am the one who worries even more.
I feel the trees whispering in my head
pushing my thoughts away:
You will touch your own heart when it is time.
Never forget that you own one in the first place.

I know the red, dense ball in my chest.
The one that I call anger, spinning
like a black hole eating all my energy.

Artemis is still there, even when I can't see her.
I hear how she exhales loudly
as if she wants to ignite a new spark in my heart:
My sweet creature, be gentle with yourself.
Allow yourself to burn. The wood can take it!

I echo as I turn back into nature.
I still have so many questions to ask.

Miriam Otto

I see you dancing
furious, wild and full of rage.

Is it because I have lost
my wild rebellious spirit
during my teenage years?

I am certain that it is you
who prevent me from finding
this part again.
Even though you love her
as much as I do.

I know, you are afraid of her.
I know, you only want to protect.
I know that you know all this.
Because you are very much part of me.

I will win my spirit back.
I wonder
what she looks like now.

To My Inner Critic

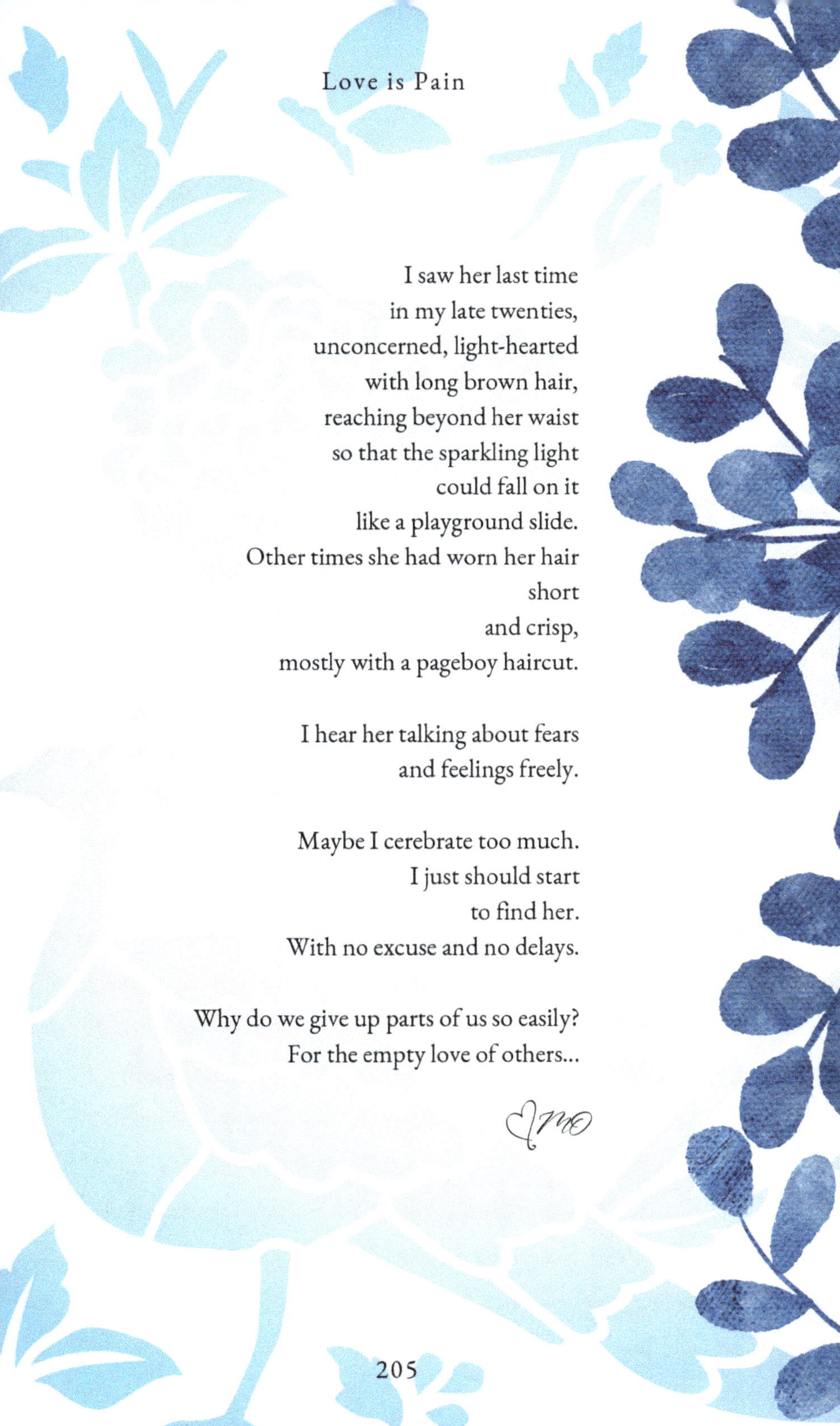

Love is Pain

I saw her last time
in my late twenties,
unconcerned, light-hearted
with long brown hair,
reaching beyond her waist
so that the sparkling light
could fall on it
like a playground slide.
Other times she had worn her hair
short
and crisp,
mostly with a pageboy haircut.

I hear her talking about fears
and feelings freely.

Maybe I cerebrate too much.
I just should start
to find her.
With no excuse and no delays.

Why do we give up parts of us so easily?
For the empty love of others...

Miriam Otto

Why Isn't There More Love in The World?

Sometimes I get affected by others,
what they think of me...

People's negative beliefs about me,
have started to become my own.

I will shake it off!
And even though,
it ripples in the cracks,
fine like sand,
it fills the holes in my scars.
Will they ever heal?
How do you heal?
One thing I know for sure,
I brush the negativity off,
shed a tear and that's it.

I will let the wind flow through me
and get rid of this painful dark magic.

Love is Pain

A blanket of stars wakes me up
in the middle of the night.

I shiver
when I realise that you are gone
and not lying beside me.

You are on your way
to new adventures.

My quilt is suitable for chilly summer days
and I am wearing less on this cold night,
not wanting the warmth and you to leave.

I see your face in front of me;
your dark brown eyes
where I am used to losing myself
within you and your love.

It is a reflection of past days,
held in my heart.

I watch the stars until they fade away
in the rising morning light
and wonder what the future will bring.

If they will whisper to me
new promises
in their silent, humming beat.

Or is it just me,
clinging to old memories
which expired long ago?

Miriam Otto

Is This Climate Change?

I have seen it with my own eyes,
autumn trees in summer.

I heard of this disease before.
Ash trees affected by a fungus, turning
yellow pale all over Italy.

I have fallen in love with
Ash leaves spreading like fingertips,
oval-shaped, like feathers on a hand.

And you ask, *Where do I find them?*

They are not many, I say.
A bit further down the hill.

They grow towards the sky,
crowns connecting the stars with dark
soil we are walking on.

And at the same time, Ash roots reach deep
until we meet the underworld.

Love is Pain

I still have hope, because I read about
some recovering in Germany.

Its firelight burns long,
a home for 1000 species.
And you ask, *Will they vanish too?*

And I say, *Maybe they will find home
in another tree.*
But I don‘t know about
the wood mice,
the bats,
some mosses,
the little blue birds
and the red bullfinch with the black head.

Tell me, I ask you, *How many Noah‘s Arks are left?*

When I Listen, Wonders Happen

Miriam Otto

Maybe this is what we call magic.

Life happens
when I step over the fine
lines of my comfort zone,
when I leave
my safe space,
when I finally use
my wings
that were clipped
for far too long.

Yellow drops fill my aches
that become healed scars
where flowers
can start to bloom,
weaving alchemy
in new beginnings.

I feel magic returning,
creating sparkling waves.

Miriam Otto

I Love You, I Think

Like a tango, the words dance with me,
full of elation,
flirting in staccato.
 Poetry sits on my shoulder as a free bird,
humming its soft melodic tunes.
 Feeling all of this, I move
my wings.

While black feathers gloom silver,
I feel the space I long for,
when we dance together.

I listen to the tragic melodies you create,
full of tensions
and promised adventures.

Is this the freedom I need?
The freedom I want?

Love is Pain

I am not sure if it will work out between
your music and me,
because I see our love drowning tragically
in your hazelnut big eyes.

I see my bird sitting on my right shoulder,
stiller then usual.
But I ignore it. I dance with you.
Because I love dancing.

Today, I feel nothing.
It is you pushing me forward.

I see the grace in your dark eyes
in which I swim
so easily,
hypnotized by your love.
I hide between the sheets of tunes,
My feathers are trimmed.
You don‘t let me fly to my own rhythm.

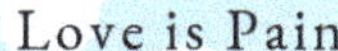

213

And yet, I keep following you.
You twist and turn me,
as if you are not sure
either.
My black bird adapts
too easily. Because she loves dancing too.

As if you can read my thoughts,
 I feel your strong,
muscular arms around my waist,
feeling safe for a minute.
And I forget about all I have thought
and what I said.

I see the smile around your eyes
playing silently while we dance.

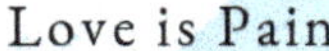

Love is Pain

Tango is a game.
I love you, I think.
Your hands so tender, searching for love.
But what love? a reminder echoes in my heart.

My poetic words and the bird,
are the soft contrast to the sad
and dramatic music
you play.
I long for wilderness. But a different one.

I hear your fast and snappy answers, as if
your vocabulary is linked to the tango as well.
You irritate me.
Why do you love me?
Is it because I dance to your music so fierce,
full of emotions,
... as it would be my last dance?

About the Author

Vaughn Roste

Canadian by birth, Vaughn Roste currently lives in Chicago. He is a published author of books, plays, poems, peer-reviewed articles, book reviews, program notes for CD liners and Carnegie Hall, and a doctoral dissertation. His first book, The *Xenophobe's Guide to the Canadians*, was published by Oval Books in England. He has two WWII films currently in pre-production, "Oradour" and "The Nine Lives of Walker Harris." His 20-min short film "Firefighter" was produced by M3 Studios and is available on You Tube, and another script entitled "Worst. Film. Ever." was purchased by Milepost42 Studios. His stage play, "The Name of The Game" won the Leo Award for Best Overall Script at the 2021 Da Vinci International Film Festival for Best Overall Script, beating out features and shorts - the first time a play has been awarded this prize. He is represented by Jason Bellitto at Citizen Skull. An optioned, represented, and produced screenwriter, Vaughn specializes in telling true stories from history with which the world should be more familiar. He is also a recovering academic, a self-confessed grammar Nazi, and has a reputation as a formatting guru. He has won 96 screenplay awards to date.

Vaughn Roste

Vaughn Roste

A Sonnet

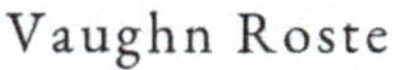

You found me once adrift, at sea, lost out on my own ocean,
a wilderness of glum despair, a cave of dark emotion.
I'm not easy to locate there, nor do I try to be,
I go to hide far deep inside for fear you might see me.

You give a hand, yet I resist, not wanting to admit
my frailty, but still I try to make the best of it.
My heart, so raw and vulnerable, screams out just to be heard,
but all I needed was that one kind, soft, supportive word.

The cracks appear in my façade, I fear the dam might break,
and I might lose all my control so precariously made.
But love will understand me and mistakes I've not yet made,
forgiveness is so painful, yet it too must work both ways.

I do not carry any more the pain that was within,
but hold so dear how you held me near - when I felt your love pour in.

The Sun Still Shines

*E*ven through the darkest storm
the sun still steadfastly shines on.
Far away, it sends its rays
to warm us every single day.

And even when we cannot see
its light, I know it's there for me.
That knowledge of sure certainty
outranks emotionality.

'Cause even when it's night outside,
the sun shines on the other side;
the globe is vast, you see, my dear -
there's sunshine somewhere, if not here.

So if you cannot see the sun
or just right now feel warmth or light,
you still yet know this too shall pass,
as day must always follow night.

Things Left Unsaid

Vaughn Roste

S'all I can manage to smile at you weakly.
Why is this stilted? We were once close.
Your eyes say more than your lips and your mouth do.
Still, it's your silence that tells me the most.
Once there was joy here, but now it's just awkward–
once there was spirit - but now only ghosts.

Three feet away, the distance enormous.
Nothing to say, yet volumes unsaid.
What I would give just to laugh again with you!
I long for days past when we were still friends...
I am still yearning that we would return there–
let me yet grieve that our laughter is dead.

I sit here mourning our journey together
quickly went south but then never got well.
I am still angry you didn't fight for us,
one-sided grief is emotional hell.
Swirling black coffee, I stir in more sugar.
The spoon in my mug pealing our sad death knell.

Love is Pain

*N*ow on our separate journeys, but
we once walked the same road -
I, cursed with heavy burden, but
you helped me share my load.

More than once I tripped and fell,
but you were there to catch me;
your reassuring presence there
both rooted and inspired me.
The path we took together led
through deepest valley yet;
but yet you never left my side -
something I won't forget.

I do not carry more that pain,
but I'll always treasure close
that it was you who helped me stand,
and how you loved me most.

Vaughn Roste

*I*t's funny—actually, far from humorous—
how the simplest things destroy me.

I can't even get groceries.

Yesterday—a single shopping cart across the lot
pierced by rude breath of winter,
alone and abandoned in soiled snow—

and I can no longer stand.

Grocery bags slip through my frail grasp,
my produce falls to earth,
because a forlorn shopping cart
struck me as a pram—
and I collapse, decimated by memory
weeping alone on cold asphalt—

bereft of hope
as the sun sets.

I wail amidst my seedless grapes
for the future stolen from me,
for my beautiful Amina—

alone and abandoned in snowy soil.

Bleak

The Past Will Not Last

Know the past
will not last.

Have no fear
for next year.

Walk away
from yesterday

to make way
for today.

Commit to grow
tomorrow.

VR

About the Author

Kelsey Annin

Kelsey Annin was born and raised in Greenville, South Carolina, where she resides with her amazing family. She has an incredibly supportive husband and two beautiful and extremely active boys. She thanks God every day for her blessings and couldn't have asked for a better family.

Kelsey has been writing since grade school and has always found creativity to be therapeutic. She finds writing to be one of the most productive ways to release a range of emotions to help her deal with life and the relationships around her. She has aspirations to publish her own books in the future, including poetry and fiction novels.

Kelsey would like to dedicate a special thanks to her mother who has always been there to correct her grammar, encourage Kelsey in her creativity, and push Kelsey to her best ability. She always believed in Kelsey, and it is because of this that she has a deep love for creativity.

I escape expressively inside the pen when I need to feel awake again.
Exploring who I am, I dig up the voluptuous lion underneath the humble lamb.
I am a wrestling warrior with ink stripes on my frenetic face.
I'm besoothed by a binding embrace as I swiftly sew the spine with grace.
Crying colors caught up in the pages with a nimble imagination untold.
I will not be silenced from myself as this sapient story unfolds.

~Kelsey Annin

Instagram: @whimsicalwisdoms_bykels

Tree of Fortitude
Shadowed Wings
Growing Pains
The Abyss of Love
Innocent Hostage
Fractured Friendship
The Epitaph of Us
Lacking Lips
Silent Streams
Boxed Identity
The Pen Made Me
Simmered Dreams
Kelsey Annin

Kelsey Annin

Your glittering rain rushes the soddened soil I step on,
exposing pregnable roots that entangle me
under the swelling weight pressing on my chest.

Above the surface, the sun paints a portrait
with a photosynthetic finish of the fruit our growth invests.

Our branches stretching to the sky,
trusting the sun to bring forth life in the blindness drawing nigh.

The fortress of this tree is one I never want to leave,
but what if these risky roots won't hold me?

KA

Tree of Fortitude

Love is Pain

She is a migrant monarch,
stretching her woven wings across sapphire skies.

From below I can see her elegant embroidery
stitched with shades of daffodil and mango.
Her framework bordered by midnight
and snowflakes peppering the edges
of her saturated soul.

I watch as she freely flies
to the tops of towering trees
searching for nectar
to nourish her crumbling confidence.

The monarch casts her shadowy silhouette
as the sun glimmers through cotton-white clouds.
She longs to be the luscious ladybug that she observes
ascending a blade of emerald green grass.
Its wings soaked in vibrant red and canvassed
with a constellation of speckled stars
across the sky of her back.

Her dreary dew drops drizzle as she yearns
to shrink herself into a smaller vessel
that can't carry the magnitude of her charm.
If only I could show her
the unique beauty she embodies,
because her eyes can't witness
the wonder in her own wings.

KA

Shadowed Wings

Kelsey Annin

Growing Pains

*H*er confidence sleeps in the grave
as grief haunts the nightmares
in the cemetery of her youth.

She stares at the dress in the closet
she can't bring herself to admit
no longer fits.

Cellulite-scented shame
washes over the skin
she no longer recognizes.

Who *defines beauty?*
What *unit measures sacrifice?*
Where *does one stop for love?*

As her moving midriff grows,
she hardly knows the power it holds
in the recesses of her mighty muscles.

God has granted her anatomy
the finesse to house human heartbeats.

Through her love,
she pumps needed nutrients
to finespun fetal bodies.

Her enveloped womb provides
a trampoline for tiny toes.

Love is Pain

With her eyesight
trapped in the magnifying glass,
she sees disagreeable stretch marks.

However, the panoramic view
shows timeless tiger stripes
that give her strength to defeat
anything motherhood might meet.

Love kindles new beginnings
as the fire from her core flames.

Her heart is wide enough
to hold the world in her vigorous veins.

Her mangled mind possesses potential
to open potent portals through agonizing pain.

Her pillowed chest provides
a comforted place to vanquish famine
and shed small sorrows.

Her laugh lines
paint magnetic memories
for those who follow.

continued

Kelsey Annin

The God of Moses has built
a formidable fortress for future generations
through her transformative body.

                She is a monument
                waiting for the sculptor
            to chisel out more definition in her skin.

                        The cartographer of her scars
                            navigates her vast voyage.

Rivers carve through weathered tears
surging directly to her spouting soul.

                The mountains she climbs,
              the valleys in which she camps,
                and the miles she treks
                are ingrained in the groves
                  of her surveyed skin.

Each wrinkle holds a story:

a smile,

                a laugh,

                              a tear.

230

Like a fine wine that betters with age,
each wrinkle brings more depth to her being
and encapsulates the richness of her memories.

If her scars could talk,
they'd tell stirring tales of a tiger
securing her staggering stripes.

Kelsey Annin

This violent void.

This graying grief.

This embowing emptiness.

It is a heavy burden
digging into the core of my battered being.
Your memory is the shovel piercing at the ground
where these salted streams fall.
In the great abyss of this darkened hole
lives every goodbye that's left my lamenting lips.

I'll guard my heart for a while and sit in this denial.
Help me paint a smile atop my tainted tears
and hide away my mangled misery.

Maybe this didn't really happen to me.

Now a red haze has my heart on fire,
and putting it out is to cut at live wire.
The mausoleum of my haltered heart
holds famished feelings unearthing me.

What can I do?

Tell me how to get a redo.

How do I move from this piercing pain?

Are these searing steps I take in vain?

For you, I'd sacrifice it all just to get another call,
because your abjuring acoustics resound beneath
the inmost shadows of my soul.

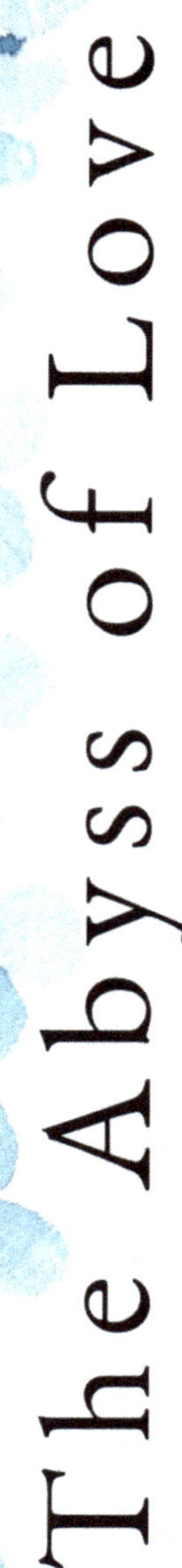

Love is Pain

She walks around him blindfolded,
avoiding his manipulative minefields.
He prefers her violable vision obscured
to hide the truth beneath his shameless shield.
Engendering precarious paths of cynicism,
he carefully leads the way,
as he blurs the gray from their play.
His fabricated pheromones oscillate,
ensuring she won't detect poisonous gas
until he lights the overpass.

He believes she's blind to his ways,
thinking of these chaptered chains as unbreakable.
Rather, inside of her lives a cultivated key,
his leavened lies no longer tasteable.
The shovel now inhabits her hands,
fooled no more by his vacillant visage.
She no longer houses her walls around him.
She refuses to be his innocent hostage.

♡ KA

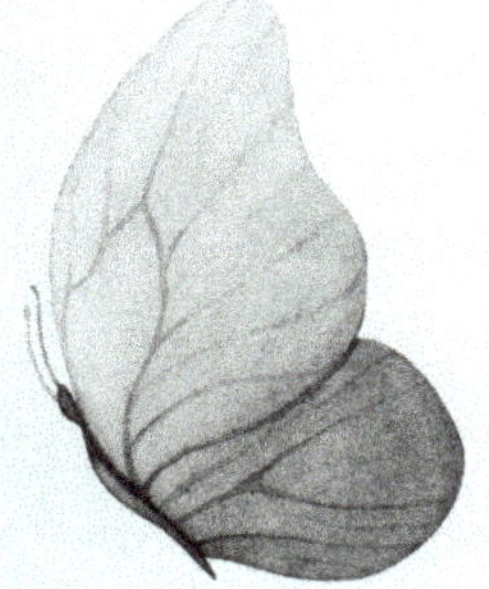

Kelsey Annin

Fractured Friendship

This is my dying request before my final words;

Make me comfortable
before putting the lifeline of our love to rest.

I beg you to be diligent
when you depart with my unmasked heart—
for I can no longer fortify my life
while it beats from the outside of my chest.

I began grieving the living
when you let yourself die to me.
Your ashes are spread across patronizing memories.

Grief doesn't walk a straight line,
so forgive me for falling behind.

Part of this splintered soul was put to bed
when you put this connection in the grave.

You didn't say goodbye
one-thousand, three-hundred, and twenty-five days ago.

Yet, no time has passed when my eyes close.

Love is Pain

You took your brush
and
painted
me
in hues of
black and white,
blotting me
from your canvas
completely.

When you put away your paint,
I no longer saw myself
in the gallery you left me in.

This hole you left behind
is a darkened void of nothingness.
I offered you all I had.

I reached out,
pouring my soul into a shattered glass.

You left me on read with my heart in limbo.

Piece by piece,

wall by wall,

door by door,

I am rebuilding my house with my own tools.

Now you're just a poem on the epitaph of my heart—
the silence you left behind is drowned out by my salt-filled song.

The Epitaph of Us

A seasonal soulmate,
A fleeting confidant,
Wallowing words won't fill
this lifeless lull left behind
on the path to our sunless cemetery.

Embalmed in flavorful fantasies,
In the crestfallen coffin
of our resplendent reveries,
I'll place these memories of you
in my second dresser drawer
to hold on a rainy day
when I need more.

The second drawer
is much larger than the top
and has more than enough room
to place the dream that is you.

This eulogy running down my cheeks
is the only way I know you were true.

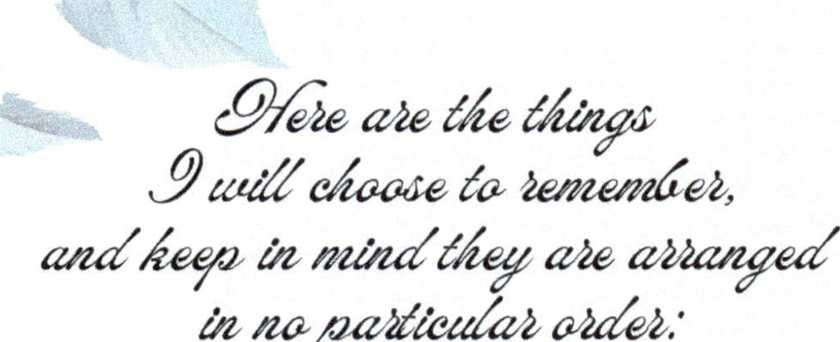

That starry night above the city
hidden away from the rest of humanity.

Road trips up winding mountain roads
to absolutely nowhere.

The smell of burning wood
as we warm our toes
in the conversation of twilight.

Midnight runs to Taco Bell as you tease me
for the rabbit food on my Crunchwrap supreme.

The sound of your voice asking me
if I made it safely home.

continued

Every stupid cat meme
that came across my phone.

The breezy eve lying in the back of your suburban
in the wooded view of the glowing moon.

The taste of your amazement when I told you
I'd never had fried pickles before I knew you.

The song of your laugh ringing in the air
as I fell into the rushing river.

The feel of warmth in our hearts
as we exchanged hopes in the nip of November.

I no longer have room in my life for regrets,
so I will follow this grave marker
to where I put us to rest.
I'll inscribe these bounties
on the time capsule of our tombstone.
I'll carry one more heartstring
before I leave this burial ground.

I hope you have a dresser drawer saved for me
where my memory can be found.

Kelsey Annin

Lacking Lips
(Tanka)

Cherry red chapstick
on your untethered work shirt.
Hold my heart closer.
Our dawning glow submerges
in luscious lips left longing.

KA

Silent Streams
(Tricube)

Rushing streams
Rivulet beams
Heart strung seams

Searing souls
Together
Taking tolls

Glimmering
Gold-specked fate
Lit too late

♡ KA

Kelsey Annin

You try to
lock me up
in your ways,

but I am
making my
quick escape.

Your toxic
ways will not
trap me in.

This box
you put me in
won't hold me back from life.
Charred chains are chiseled from my wrists,
writhing.

I am creating,
owning the shape my life takes.
Flirting with this pen,
I'll carve my poetry path.
My feet will take back control.

Boxed Identity

Love is Pain

For I no longer follow your rules,
and never again will I be bound
by the pages you wrote me on.
I'll count to my heart's tempo
and draw my own alluring adjectives.
I'll rhyme lashful lyrics in my own time.

My pen has been released
to paint my own analogies,
away from forced apologies.

I've found a voice veering so far
it echoes exigently above forlorn lies.
With the paint I mix together,
I will color the imagery
of you how I see it from my eyes.

For I no longer follow your rules
and will never again be bound
by the pages you wrote me on.

You tried to lock me up,
but
I have made
this life line up
how I see fit.

Kelsey Annin

Ink runs through the veins of my memories,
Skillfully burning at my fingertips.
With her grip, the plotting pen steals this tale.
Puddles of tears poor pages of rages.
My trauma was not ever invited,
yet, even so, the pen made me write it.

I know I promised I wouldn't spill it,
but how do I wipe mere memories?
These lethal words are ones you invited.
Rashly, you threw them at slick fingertips.
Now this pen is grabbing all my rages
and plagiarizing this unruly tale.

Please don't blame me for spoiling this tale,
The pen sees a story and follows it.
I know when the truth shows you your rages,
you'll convince me these aren't real memories.
That these smudges aren't from your fingertips,
and I'm the one that trauma invited.

Which of you has asked who I've invited?
When will I own this treacherous tale?
The pen has cemented my fingertips.
All along the pen secretly knew it
and wanted truth in these sly memories
to act as a witness to your rages.

The Pen Made Me
(Sestina)

The pen takes me away from your rages
and records them the way I've invited,
taking back meticulous memories
before you sell me a strained pseudo-tale,
so you can't take the eraser to it
and wash away your feral fingertips.

I've loosened my tie from your fingertips.
Now I'm the one filled with these red rages.
Yes, your gas lit path led me right to it.
Why would you ever think you're invited?
You won't pass the paper that shares this tale.
This pen has sipped up these memories.

These memories, these furtive fingertips,
I've tucked away these tales in my rages.
Seems I've invited the pen to write it.

Kelsey Annin

Do I exist in your deep-seated dreams
like a vicious volcano boiling to the surface?
Have you silenced the danger searing at the seams
leaving me to fry in this fiery furnace?

Like a vicious volcano boiling to the surface,
heat rises in your lethal lava,
leaving me to fry in this fiery furnace,
simmering in your half-baked karma.

Heat rises in your lethal lava.
Have you silenced the danger searing at the seams,
simmering in your half-baked karma?
Do I exist in your deep-seated dreams?

♡ KA

Simmered Dreams
(A Pantoum)

Poetry Formats

Cinquain: A five-lined poem that utilizes a 2, 4, 6, 8, 2 syllabic pattern for a total of 22 syllables in the whole piece. This diamond-shaped poetry form originated in America after being inspired by the Japanese Haiku (5, 7, 5).

Pantoum: A fixed poetic form that uses a specific repetition of each line to create a sort of pendulum effect. By the end of the poem, the pattern will have each line repeated twice. This style began in France.

Sestina: A fixed form of poetry that utilizes a unique repetition of ending words in each stanza. It contains seven stanzas. Six of the stanzas have six lines and the final stanza has three lines. This style began in Italy and France and is typically written in iambic pentameter.

Tanka: A five-lined poem that utilizes a 5, 7, 5, 7, 7 syllabic pattern for a total of 31 syllables in the whole piece. This form of poetry originated in Japan.

Tricube: A three-stanza poem. Each stanza contains three lines following a triple meter, or three-syllable lines, to create three "cubes". This type of ancient poetry was utilized to pass on oral songs, chants, and prayers.

Kelsey's poem "Boxed Identity" includes a Tricube, Cinquain, and a Tanka before breaking out into free form to emphasize finding freedom in one's identity.

About the Author

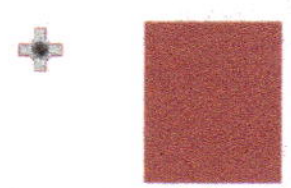

Stevie Flood

Residing on the beautiful Maltese Islands, Stevie Flood has captivated most of her magnificent essence in writing, by the attention of no other than the landscapes alone. Seasonal changes on the island bring out her colourful pieces of ink to light.

At the ripe old age of four, Stevie began her literacy journey. Very special thanks to her father, Peter Flood, who always encouraged her on a whole other level – to be inspired by the outside world around her, and detail it to its very core of how magnificent ink could be, if it is described down to the very last drop of ink, in her mind only then the story will be complete.

Making her life as full as can be, these fine pieces of ink were motivated by unfortunate events, and now slowly shimmering memories remain of the man she writes her pieces to. If you would love to find out more and read more of her amazing poetry, just look her up on:

Facebook at: https://www.facebook.com/stevie.floodauthor/
Instagram: https://www.instagram.com/stevie.flood/
TikTok: https://www.tiktok.com/@stevieflood4

The Day To Wed Is Now Dead

Letters Left Unsent

The Bird's Last Song

Billions

Loving Amid Ghosting
Confessions

The Storm (prose)

The Storm (poem)

Never Forgotten,
Never Erased

The Heart's Whale Cry

The Day Is Gone

The Heartbreak of a Broken Heart

Love is a Battlefield

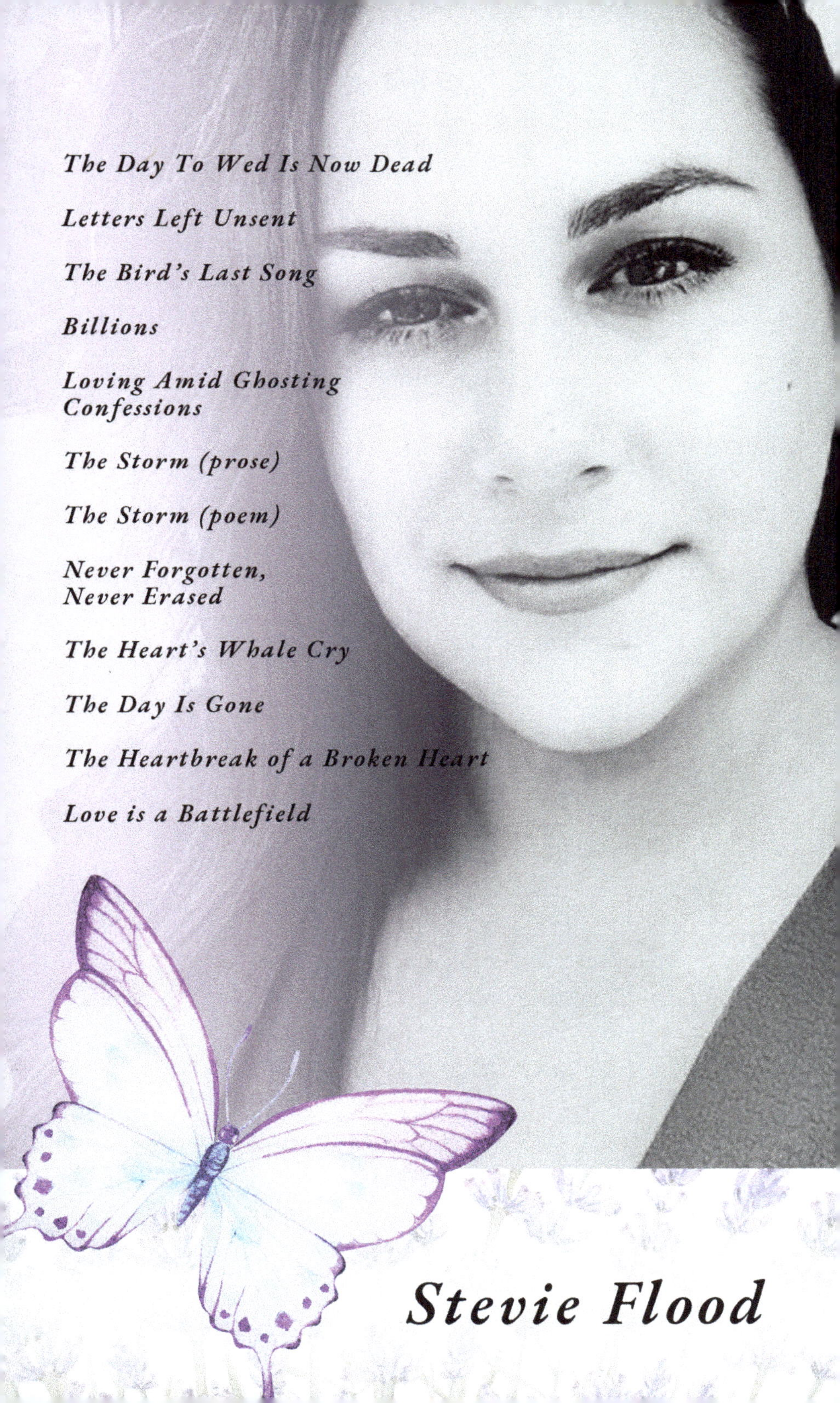

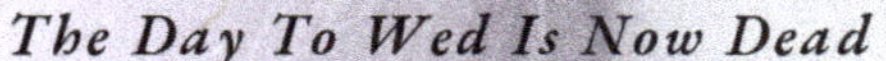

Stevie Flood

The Day to Wed is Now Dead

Stevie Flood

In the garden of promises, wilted and gray,
the day to wed, a ghost, now fades away.
Once vibrant blooms, a tapestry of hope,
now draped in shadows, a desolate slope.

Beneath the mourning sky, where dreams were sown,
echoes linger, a symphony of vows—overthrown.
The altar, adorned with dreams untold,
now crumbles, a relic of love grown cold.

The day to wed, now entombed in sorrow,
a melancholy anthem for a heart to borrow.
The veil of joy, once lifted high,
is now shrouded in the tears of a desolate sky.

The hymn of love, a requiem unsung,
in the ruins of promises, where echoes clung.
The dance of two souls, a fleeting waltz,
now a solitary figure in somber vaults.

Gone is the laughter, the jubilant cheer,
replaced by silence, a sepulchral sphere.
The vows, once whispered in the sacred hush,
now echo in the void, a ghostly hush.

Love is Pain

The day to wed, a relic entwined with dread,
a tale untold, a love thread now unwed.
Memories linger in the empty hall,
the ghost of love, a mournful pall.

As twilight weaves its melancholy spell,
the day to wed in a sepulcher does dwell.
The embers of hope, now a fading ember,
in the mausoleum of love's lost November.

Yet, in the quiet of this funereal gloom,
a whisper lingers, a bud in the tomb.
For love's requiem, though heavy with lead,
may birth anew from the day that's dead.

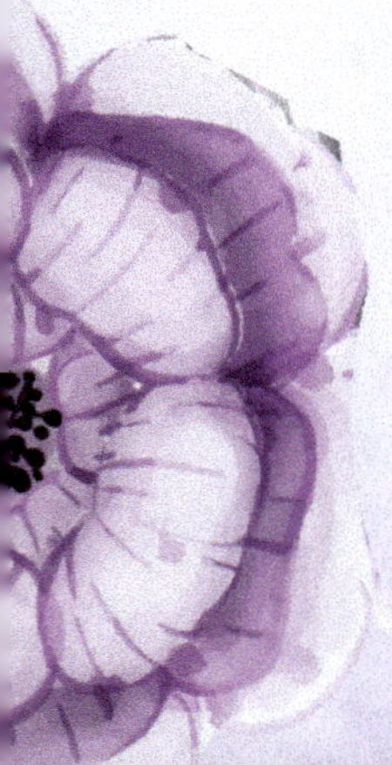

Letters Left Unsent

In the vast tapestry of human existence, amidst the countless chapters that unfold in the journey of life, there exists a poignant and profound phenomenon known as "letters left unsent."

These letters, tenderly composed and laden with the weight of raw emotions, remain unshared, locked away in the secret chambers of the heart.

They embody a unique blend of vulnerability, courage, and hesitancy, encapsulating the unspoken stories and unexpressed sentiments that reverberate within the human soul.

Each unsent letter represents a chapter in the symphony of human emotions, an intricate dance between the desire to communicate and the fear of vulnerability.

They are a testament to the art of restraint, where words are penned with great care, only to be tucked away and shielded from the prying eyes of the world.

These letters could be expressions of love that bloom like fragile flowers in the garden of the heart, but their petals remain delicately closed, unable to embrace the warmth of the sun.

Some of these letters are the embodiment of forgiveness, where the writer yearns to absolve old wounds and foster reconciliation, yet hesitates to take that decisive step forward.

Others may bear the weight of gratitude, a fervent desire to extend appreciation and acknowledgment to a recipient who, for various reasons, remains unaware of the writer's profound gratitude.

continued

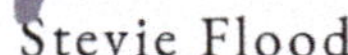

Within the realm of letters left unsent, there are the elegies of sorrow—addressed to beloved souls who have departed this mortal coil. In the wake of loss—the longing to say a final farewell, to capture the essence of a cherished relationship one last time— echoes throughout the ethereal parchment. Yet, fate intervenes, leaving these letters as poignant echoes of eternal love and remembrance, forever cherished in the heart's sacred sanctum.

The enigmatic allure of these unposted letters lies in their ability to transcend time and space—remaining relevant even as days turn into years. They are preserved fragments of a moment's sincerity, crystallized emotions that capture the essence of a particular juncture in the writer's life. Perhaps they are letters of confession, where secrets too heavy to bear are relinquished onto paper—not with the intention of sending them, but with the hope of finding solace in their release.

While these letters might never reach their intended recipients, their significance should not be underestimated. For they serve as a testament to the intricate tapestry of human relationships, where words left unsaid can carry as much power as those that find their way to the intended audience. They symbolize the complexity of human nature, the interplay of emotion and reason, and the inescapable truth that vulnerability lies at the core of meaningful connections.

In the end, letters left unsent are a treasure trove of untold stories and unshared sentiments. They stand as a testament to the courage it takes to open one's heart and the beauty of unspoken words that transcend the limitations of language. Like uncut gems, they remain pristine in their unexpressed form, a reflection of the intricate dance between our desires to connect and our hesitations to reveal the depths of our souls.

The Bird's Last Song

Stevie Flood

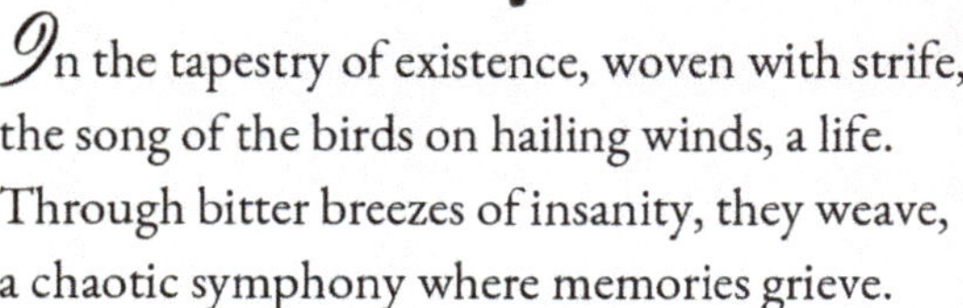

In the tapestry of existence, woven with strife,
the song of the birds on hailing winds, a life.
Through bitter breezes of insanity, they weave,
a chaotic symphony where memories grieve.

In the realm where avian melodies once soared,
now, a cacophony of discord, feelings implored.
Winds rustling with tales of forsaken yore,
in the bitter breeze, sanity's whispers—ignored.

The birds' song now echoes on tumultuous gales,
a chorus entangled in life's chaotic trails.
Their feathers brushed by winds of fleeting sanity
lost in the tempest: a poignant calamity.

In the hailing winds, whispers of remembrance,
a dance with shadows, a haunting semblance.
Forlorn in the grasp of a relentless storm,
life's melody weaves a tapestry, forlorn.

To remember, a pilgrimage through the echoes,
to forget is an elusive pursuit that life bestows.
In the bitter breeze, where chaos entwines,
memories unravel where the heart defines.

Love is Pain

Each note of the birds, a reverie untold
in the chaos, memories and dreams unfold.
Forlorn, we stand in the tempest's eye,
a blend of remembering and bidding goodbye.

In the tapestry's threads, woven with despair,
the birds' song lingers as a spectral prayer.
Hailing winds carry tales of both regret and bliss
in the bitter breeze—life's chaotic abyss.

Yet within the chaos, resilience blooms
as the birds' song persists in turbulent rooms.
To remember and forget: a dual decree,
in life's bitter breeze, a poignant symphony.

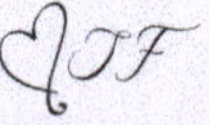

Stevie Flood

$\mathcal{S}$imultaneously, in the vast expanse of existence, billions of lives cease to persist. A profound silence envelops the cosmos as individuals breathe their final breaths, their narratives concluding in the silent dance of mortality.

In the hushed corridors of existence, countless thoughts linger unspoken, echoing in the spaces between stars, a cosmic symphony of unuttered expressions that fade into the cosmic background. Alongside the extinguished flames of lives, billions of dreams linger in the ethereal realm of the unfulfilled. They cast shadows in the tapestry of human potential, suspended in the delicate balance between aspiration and the inexorable passage of time.

Unseen and unheard, these dreams carry the weight of the unrealized, leaving a poignant resonance in the vast emptiness of ...

what could have been.

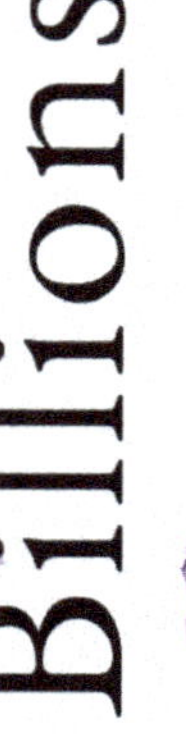

Billions

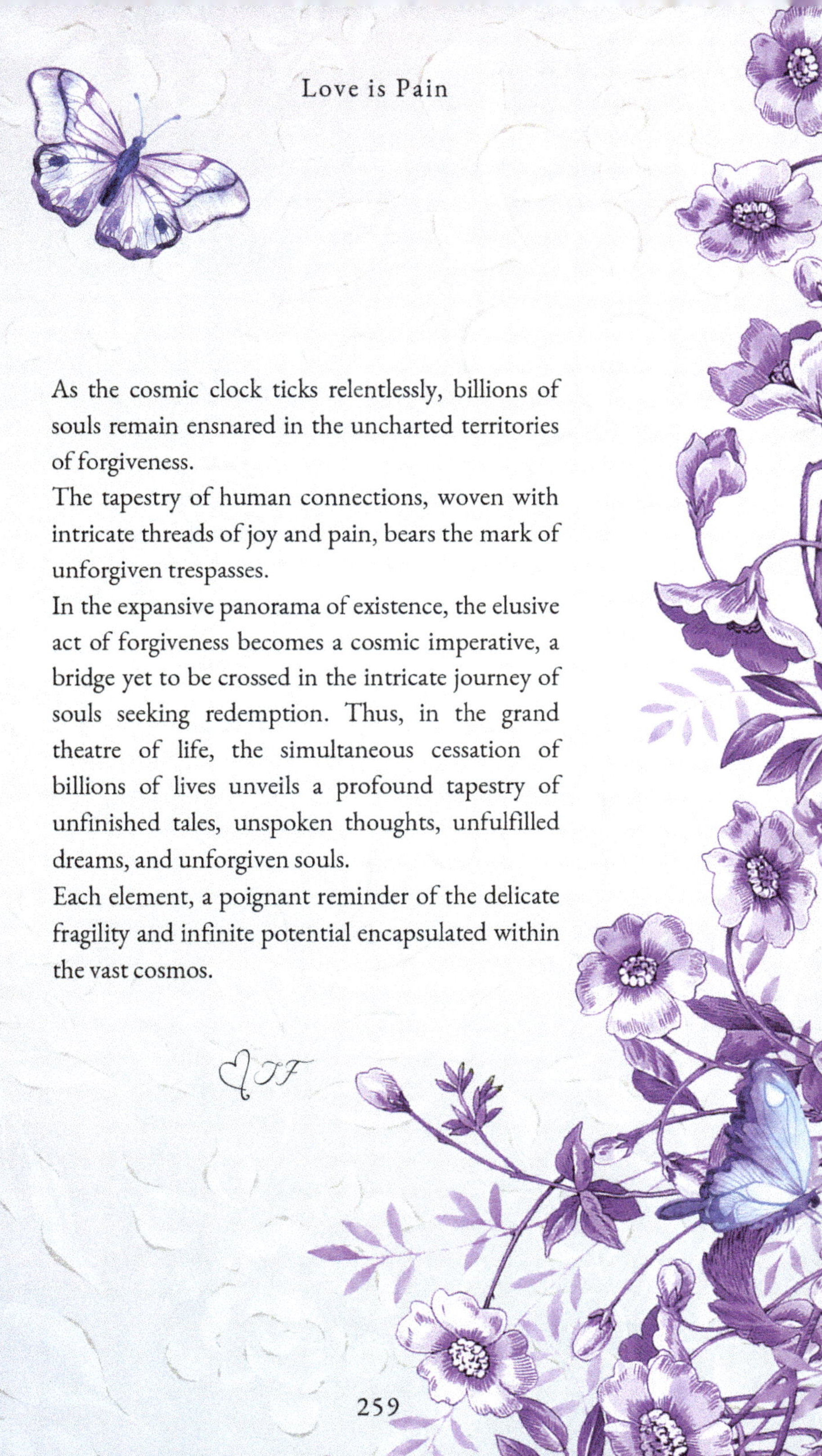

As the cosmic clock ticks relentlessly, billions of souls remain ensnared in the uncharted territories of forgiveness.

The tapestry of human connections, woven with intricate threads of joy and pain, bears the mark of unforgiven trespasses.

In the expansive panorama of existence, the elusive act of forgiveness becomes a cosmic imperative, a bridge yet to be crossed in the intricate journey of souls seeking redemption. Thus, in the grand theatre of life, the simultaneous cessation of billions of lives unveils a profound tapestry of unfinished tales, unspoken thoughts, unfulfilled dreams, and unforgiven souls.

Each element, a poignant reminder of the delicate fragility and infinite potential encapsulated within the vast cosmos.

Stevie Flood

Loving Amid Ghosting Confessions

In shadows' embrace my heart did quiver,
confessions of love, a silent river.
He, a specter in the mists of yore,
his absence—a haunting I couldn't ignore.

On moonlit nights, his memory's art
whispered sweetly to my lonely heart.
A love, once bloomed, vibrant, and fair,
now echoes faintly in the chilled night air.

Through unseen words and ghostly presence,
I cradled dreams lost in essence.
Invisible threads he gently wove,
his vanishing act; my heart's trove.

Yet, love persevered through vacant space;
a flickering flame in the desolate place.
Whispers of adoration unheard, unseen—
haunted my thoughts in shades of green.

The unanswered calls, the messages lost.
A labyrinth of feelings, an emotional cost.
Yet, love's ember glowed deep within,
unfazed by the ghostly silent din.

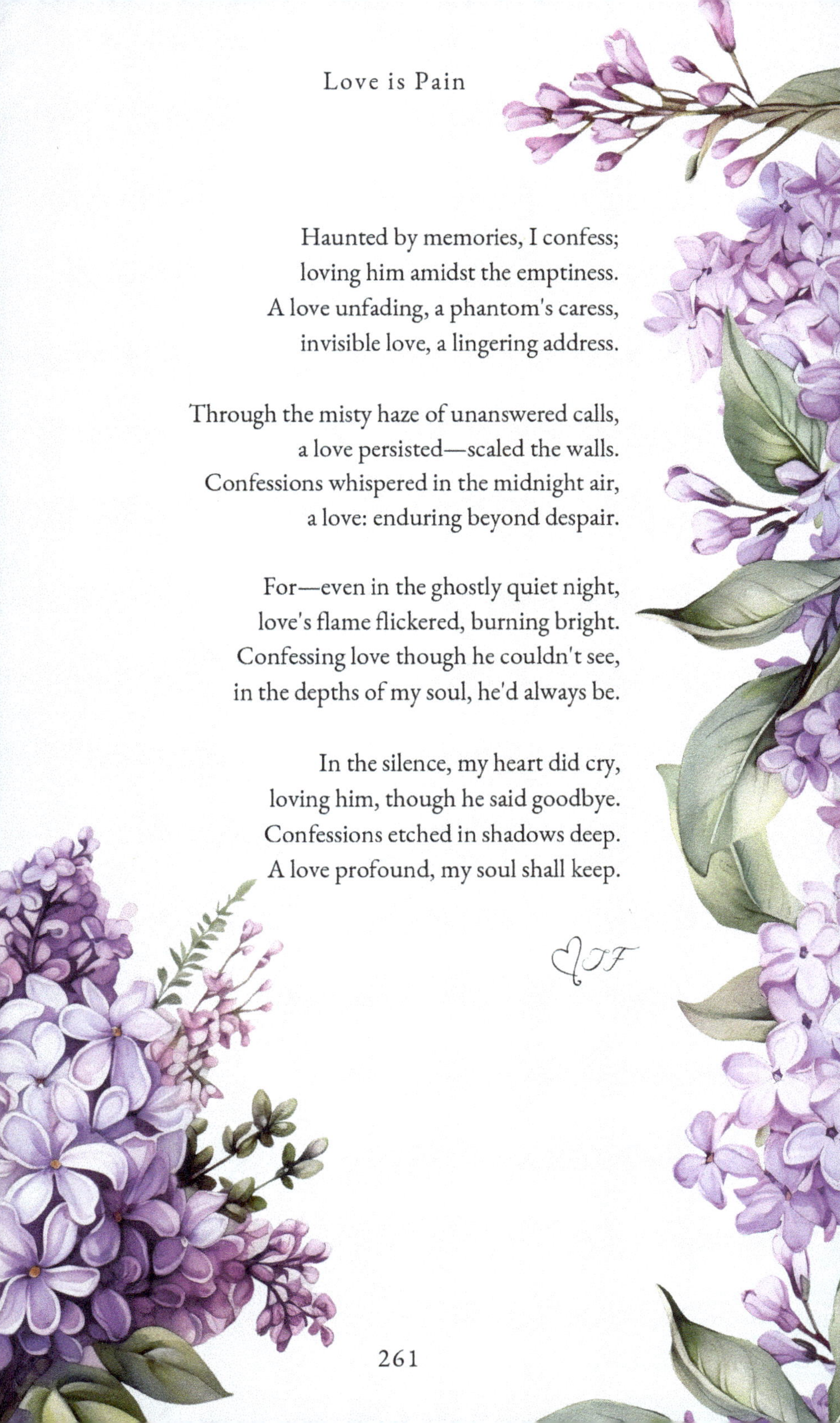

Love is Pain

Haunted by memories, I confess;
loving him amidst the emptiness.
A love unfading, a phantom's caress,
invisible love, a lingering address.

Through the misty haze of unanswered calls,
a love persisted—scaled the walls.
Confessions whispered in the midnight air,
a love: enduring beyond despair.

For—even in the ghostly quiet night,
love's flame flickered, burning bright.
Confessing love though he couldn't see,
in the depths of my soul, he'd always be.

In the silence, my heart did cry,
loving him, though he said goodbye.
Confessions etched in shadows deep.
A love profound, my soul shall keep.

Stevie Flood

If there are moments in a lifetime that one could share, it would be the moment that I lost absolutely everything to the fiery rain that poured down on me the day I lost you.

Many people think that this is an open letter, but I have to admit that it's not. I've had multiple dreams along the days that you have departed this life and imagined what life would have been like if you were still in it.

Dreary rain continues to pour down on top of my head, and yet I still remember that crash of lightning that struck just five minutes after I awoke from a deep sleep, feeling your hand wrapped around me on that bed where we lay.

Though time does heal, it also shows that feelings are pretty much like the weather; we reach our anger like storms that are yet to be foreseen in years to come. We smile like the sun is shining down on us, and we tend to cry like the rain has come down multiple times. Yet, just like the wind, we are not seen, but we are heard.

Some are heard in the silence of the stillness outside when the branches of the trees start swerving; others are just like hypnotic trends that we can call a tornado warning. This warning sign is a wailing sound that screams out all silences. It's the wailing of the wind that we feel around us when we are not looking. And most of all, it's the feeling within us that releases every particle of that pain that we have lost over the years.

It pretty much sounds like a typical piece of work, huh? Well, I guess Mother Nature wasn't put together in one day, was it? I believe that she continues to grow as we evolve, and at some point, when that barrier breaks, all hell will break the mercy that comes between me and my feelings.

Love is Pain

*I*n moments shared through a lifetime's thread,
lost utterly to fiery rain, where love had bled;
not an open letter, I confess, it's true,
dreams dance with echoes, days without you.

In the drizzle of dreams, you've left behind
a bed where we once, in love, entwined.
Dreary rain continues; a ceaseless pour,
I recall the lightning striking at my core.

Time, a healer, whispers tales untold—
yet feelings, like weather in stories unfold.
Anger storms unforeseen in Future's gaze,
smiles like the sun casting warmth ablaze.

Crying, akin to rain; multiple times it falls—
as the wind, unseen but in its echoing calls.
Whispers in stillness, trees' branches swaying,
a tornado warning, hypnotic trends playing.

The wailing sound, a warning clear—
silence breaking, winds drawing near.
Mother Nature was not built in one day.
Evolution's dance, emotions at play.

Breaking barriers, unleashing pain's decree,
Hell may break, but mercy sets feelings free.
In the dance of growth, nature, and soul entwined,
a symphony of emotions, evolving, undefined.

JF

The Storm (as poem)

Never Forgotten, Never Erased

Stevie Flood

In the tapestry of time where memories reside,
a refrain echoes a promise to abide.
Never forgotten, engraved in the heart's embrace,
a testament enduring, leaving no trace.

Through the corridors of days, echoes persist,
whispers of moments in time's gentle mist.
Faces and places in memory's sacred space,
never forgotten—held in a cherished embrace.

Footprints in the sands of both joy and strife.
A vow, unspoken yet echoing through life.
Never erased, the imprints of the past,
in the heart's gallery, they'll forever last.

Like stars in the night, their brilliance remains,
a constellation of love that nothing restrains.
Never forgotten, though the years may unfold,
in the stories untold, their presence is told.

In the quiet moments, when shadows fall,
the never-forgotten echoes softly call.
A bond unbroken, a connection, unswayed;
never erased, in the heart's serenade.

Through the ebb and flow of life's changing tide,
the never-forgotten echoes, side by side.
A melody of love, in eternal grace,
never erased, an enduring embrace.

The Heart's Whale Cry

Beneath the vast expanse of midnight's sea,
a heart's lament unfolds in a mournful plea.
echoes of sorrow, like a whale's deep cry, were a
symphony of longing beneath the starry sky.

In the ocean of silence, where shadows roam,
a heart's whaling sound; an ancient, somber poem.
Like a whale's song, haunting and profound,
lost in the depths, where emotions are found.

A melody of ache, rhythmic despair,
the heart's wailing—a burden it must bear.
Each note is a ripple in the ocean of night,
a lamentation that seeks solace in starlight.

The echoes resonate, a forlorn refrain,
as the heart's whale cry navigates the pain.
Through the currents of longing, it reverberates
a serenade of sorrow that silently narrates.

In the vastness of emotions where depths conceal,
the heart's whaling song, a truth it reveals.
A dance with echoes in the vast, cosmic sea,
a melancholy melody of a soul's decree.

*I*n the fading hues of the day's embrace,
love's tale unfolds a bittersweet grace.
The sun retreats, leaving shadows to reign,
a canvas painted, where love is pain.

The daylight wanes, a whispered adieu,
yet, in the twilight, love's residue.
Aching hearts, in the dusky light,
lost in the echoes of a waning fight.

The colors fade, like love's refrain,
a symphony of longing, a quiet disdain.
As stars emerge in the darkened sky,
love's silent tears, in the night, comply.

With each passing moment, a subtle ache,
love's complexity, no words can make.
In the stillness of the night's domain,
whispers linger, where love is pain.

Moonlight weaves tales of aching hearts,
a poignant melody as the night imparts.
Yet, in the shadows, love remains,
a paradox of joy entwined with chains.

So, as the day surrenders its light,
love's enigma deepens in the quiet night.
In every goodbye, a lingering refrain,
for in love's essence, there's beauty in pain.

SF

The Day is Gone

Love is Pain

The Heartbreak of a Broken Heart

In the radiance of life, a heartache unfolds.
In broken hearts, stories remain untold.
Morning's light draped in a somber sheen.
A tapestry of pain, where wounds convene.

Each sunrise whispers of love that's amiss,
unmended hearts in the dawn's cold kiss.
The canvas of hope, now painted with tears—
a symphony of sorrow echoing through the years.

Dreary morn unfolds a solemn decree
where fractured dreams dwell endlessly.
Hearts denied the chance to find reprieve
in the shadowed corridors, where echoes deceive.

Through the radiance of joy, a darkness weaves—
in the shattered pieces, a soul bereaves.
Torn asunder, the fabric of trust,
on this dreary morn, love lies in the dust.

Unspoken words linger in morning's mist,
a poignant reminder of the love dismissed.
Unmended hearts ache in silent refrain,
in the radiance of life, where shadows stain.

Yet, amidst the brokenness, resilience gleams,
hope flickers faintly in shattered dreams.
For even in heartache's relentless grip,
a strength emerges, refusing to slip.

In the dreary morn, as sunlight wanes,
Hearts may find solace in gentle rains.
For life's broken pieces, though scattered and torn,
Hold the promise of a mending, a new morn.

Stevie Flood

Love Is A Battlefield

In the heart's arena,
love takes its stand;
a battlefield
where passions command.

With every glance,
a skirmish ignites,
as hearts entwine
in fierce, fervent fights.

But when love shatters,
it's a war untamed,
leaving scars where once
affection flamed.

Emotions bleed
across the fields of strife,
in the wreckage of
what was once life.

Each tear shed
is a drop of crimson hue,
in the blood-soaked soil
where dreams once grew.

Love is Pain

Yet amidst the chaos,
hope may arise,
as wounded souls seek solace
'neath the skies.

For from the ashes,
new strength may be found,
in the courage to heal
on battlegrounds unwound.

Though love may falter,
and hearts may yield,
in the aftermath,
new love may be revealed.

About the
Author/Curator/ Editor

Brandy Lane

Brandy Lane has lived most of her life in Indiana and Colorado. She published her first book, *Where Beautiful Loves*, in December 2020 under her imprint Where Beautiful Inks. Just after the release of her first book, she discovered anthologies as an option for publishing and has since had poetry pieces included in over three dozen publications. Publications include *Poetry 365 by RDW* (both abridged and unabridged editions) for November, December, January, February, March, April, May, and June, and special editions of *Creator* and *Self Portrait* editions. Red Penguin Books has published her pieces in *'Tis the Season's*, *The Flower Shop on the Corner*, and *The Ocean Waves*. Clarendon House Publications published her poems in their *Poetica 2* and *Poetica 3* anthologies, and her work was also included in Ink Gladiator's Press anthologies of *The Rise and Fall of Chimera's* and *Gray, We Hide our Colors Within*. Indie Blu(e) Publishing just published a mental health piece in *Through the Looking Glass: Reflecting on Madness and Chaos Within*, and their newest anthology, *But You Don't Look Sick*. 300 South Media Group has published her in *As Darkness Falls, Shadow of the Soul*, and features her first flash fiction piece in *Sunset Rain*. Train River Poetry has published her in *Poetry 7*. She also appears in *Who's Who of Emerging Writers* by Sweetycat Press. Most recently, she has been published by *Harness Magazine* in their November issue, and Silent Spark Press *Amazing Poetry*. Brandy can be found online: on Instagram and Facebook @wherebeautifullives.

Don't Let Me Go

This Heart of Mine

Diamonds

Tangible

Spark

Fallen World

Conundrum

For Daphne

Wailing Woman

Bites Like Peppers

Whene'er

Your Arms Around Me

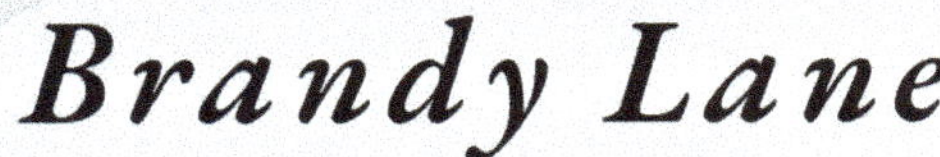

Brandy Lane

Brandy Lane

Don't Let Me Go

Can you talk to me like you used to,
just for a night?
Can you put your arms around me
and hug me real tight?

And don't ever let me go?

♡ BL

Love is Pain

This heart of mine can't bear much more,
I want to run and never look back.
My heart aches inside this hollow chest,
feels like a massive heart attack.

I've tried to hang on for so long,
through years of chaos I've traveled.
All the strings, incessantly pulled,
has made my soul unraveled.

I no longer care about,
oh, so many things.
Because of all the disappointment
this situation brings.

I have learned that hope is fleeting,
that joy is not something that stays.
and I cannot sit and ponder
those now distant days.

All I know is my future,
no longer looks so bright.
And hope—my only moon,
in this dark, cold night.

*T*here are no more poems here.

They left with the faded memories of you.
I can no longer remember your touch,
your glance, your smile.

In photographs, you look
just like everyone else, and I feel
the reminiscence of everything about you—
being sucked out of my mind;
like a dementor would a wizard's soul.

I miss the high, but I certainly *don't* miss
the soul-crushing lows, the withdrawal
that I went through when you quit texting me—
when you emotionally closed yourself off.

Part of me *wants* to miss you,
but it hurts too much.
Part of me wants to see you again;
like an alcoholic misses the wine
but then remembers the headaches
that follow inevitably
the next morning.

Love is Pain

I miss being *that* happy.
I will probably *never* be that happy again.
Those beautiful moments I had when I knew—
dammit when I KNEW you loved me—
will haunt me like a tune;
stuck in my head for eternity.

I still love you, and that I cannot deny. But you
are the one that gave up. YOU, not me. I waited
for you, hoped you'd fight for me, knowing
that I was under a spell—trapped in a tower.
I would've run to you had I had the chance.

I guess this fairy tale has ended,
but I never got my happily ever after, and
frankly... I don't want one.

I don't want to ever feel the way I felt about
you with anybody else. I'd rather have this
empty, hollow feeling, like half of me is missing
than try to fill it with whatever tries to replace
what I had with you.

I'd rather have these diamonds pour from my
eyes than have them placed in another crown.
I was your princess, you were my dragon.
I will always remember you that way.

Brandy Lane

$\mathcal{I}$f there were a signal,
much like how Batman had,
for all of the men and women who
have finally made the decision to leave;
I wonder how many beacons
would be in the sky tonight?

I wonder if there was a way
to make it visible to everyone,
to make it tangible,
if anyone would come to help?

Wouldn't it be amazing?
To be able to shine that light,
and have a crew of people
ready to help you through that door?

I'm curious as to how many
are suffering in silence,
just like me.

BL

Tangible

Spark

I'm not sure how or why it happened,
but tonight I found my way back.
I'm writing this while lucid,
while I can still feel everything.

For about an hour now,
I have been able to dream,
to think, to laugh, to feel.

I have been able to imagine and to love.

I'm so afraid it is going to fade again,
this feeling that makes me who I am,
that spark that gives me hope for the future,
the one that reminds me
that I can make a difference.

♡ BL

Brandy Lane

In this fallen world, we are as clover, struggling to grow in the cracks of the concrete. Reaching for the sun and trying not to be trampled by hurried feet.

Begging—to be seen, lest we be nibbled up by Lagamorphs or tickled by Lepidoptera's tiny feet.

I see you over there and continue to cheer you on— although I, too, am waist-deep in ash, gravel, and chewed-up blobs of gum, all over these big city streets.

Feeling discarded when alone, trying to tell myself I'm somehow important while looking at every other human speck on the planet, feeling small—at least, until I remember all in this together.

That was the key that I lost along the path, the key that took me outside of my own self-pity, the one that opens the door to joy and empathy.

The one that reminds me: that I am not alone.

♡ BL

Love is Pain

Does everyone feel as awkward as I do in my own skin?
Am I blind to what everyone else sees?
Because when I look in the mirror,
I don't always see a woman.
No, I just see my soul wrapped in a flesh burrito.

Some days, I see a beautiful girl, others...
a disgusting blob, a mess.
This morning, I felt more masculine.

I stared into my fresh face and wondered
if I would be seen any differently
without mascara or a bra.
I wondered if I would be able to handle my life better
if I approached it as a man—
as someone who is not always seen as a victim, as frail.
Not as someone who "should be seen and not heard,"
as it was ingrained in my head as a child.

I wondered how the complexities of life
have led me to this conundrum.
Knowing who I am inside,
yet never being allowed to be myself.
Only one person has ever seen the real me...
and he knows that I am trapped in a world
where I am not supposed to be.

So many people have left me to myself.
This monster I've become, with no love left to give.
I gave all of it away to someone
who will never be mine.

Conundrum

Brandy Lane

You are most lovely of the flowers
standing straight and tall,
trying so hard to reach the sun
before your petals fall.

You close up all around yourself
so e'en the moon can't see
that you are so very full
of vulnerability.

At night is where I find you,
all bound up in frailty.
I'll sit beside you as the moon
shines down on you and me.

I'll stay with you until you want
to open up again,
and even when you're silent,
I will sit with you, my friend.

280

Love is Pain

I look forward to the day,
I can watch you bloom once more,
and tending to your garden, well -
has never been a chore.

the wind and rain will pour down
with lightning and its thunder,
and the love I have for you
let no one put asunder.

For you, it turns out, are the rose,
all delicate and such...
and me? I'm just the gardener,
who cherishes you much.

Wailing Woman

There's a wailing woman inside of me;
she makes my heart hurt quite often.
She screams sometimes,
and I'm not quite sure
how she got there.
I can never tame her,
so I keep her locked away.

She is wild.
She loves without restrictions.
She wants to drink a little too much.
She laughs a little too loud.
She aches for the ones she cannot have.
If I don't shut her up
she will ruin the life I have built—
the carefully-placed Jenga blocks,
precariously tall.

That woman rants from inside her cage
my ribs contain her rage.
Sometimes you can hear her under my breath.
The few times I have set her free:
She made all the wrong decisions.
Because I didn't shut her up
she got hurt—
she ruined the life I could've had,
a sturdy one, secure.

Love is Pain

That woman is knocking again...
she wants to come out.
I cannot always tell if it is her knocking,
or if it's just my heart beating.

Maybe I should set her free?
She might have learned her lesson!
She might surprise me!
She might make things exciting!

she might make everything better
she might be right.
What if she isn't though?
What if I have to lock her away again?
What if she makes things worse?
What if I shouldn't let her speak her mind?
What If she's wrong?
There's a wailing woman inside of me,
she makes my heart hurt quite often.
She screams sometimes,
and I'm not sure how she got there.
I can never tame her,
so I keep her locked away...

♡ BL

283

Brandy Lane

*I*n the bitter melancholy of morning
the sun bites my skin like hot peppers,
stings my eyes, and causes me to sneeze.

Remembering you causes the same reaction.
'Cept my skin tingles with delight,
as if ghosts are whispering in my ear
and teasing my body suit with their breath.

My eyes sparkle, wet with tears,
regretting the moments
I've missed alongside you
because of my past decisions.

I don't sneeze but smother my face in my blanket;
so no one hears the howling of my broken heart,
so no one sees how very much this hurts
not having you in my life.

♡ BL

I hope the tides of change
come, and sweep you away
to places you never dreamed
you'd meander to.

**I pray you always smile
whene'er you think of me.**

♡ *BL*

Your Arms Around Me

I put on a shirt...
then put on a sweater,
made me feel warmer,
though not that much better.

I sat in a chair—
wrapped myself in a throw.
Something's still missing,
but what's that? I don't know.

The coffee is made
the light's filtering in
on this gorgeous day
that's beck'ning to begin.

I'm just not content
and I fear I won't be
'til the day that I have
your arms around me.

fin

Other books by Brandy Lane:

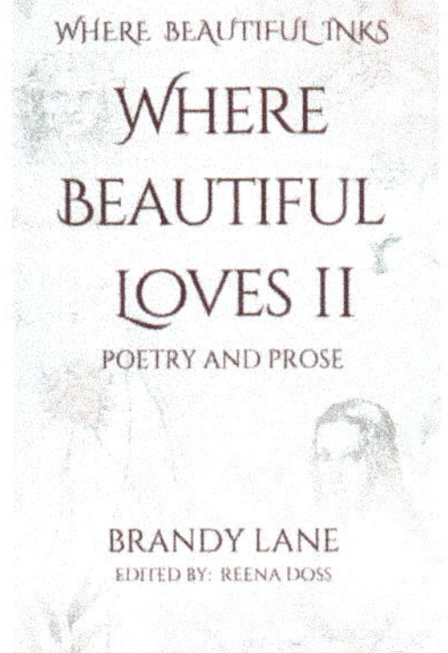

Other anthologies by Where Beautiful Inks

In the Works

ANTHOLOGIES

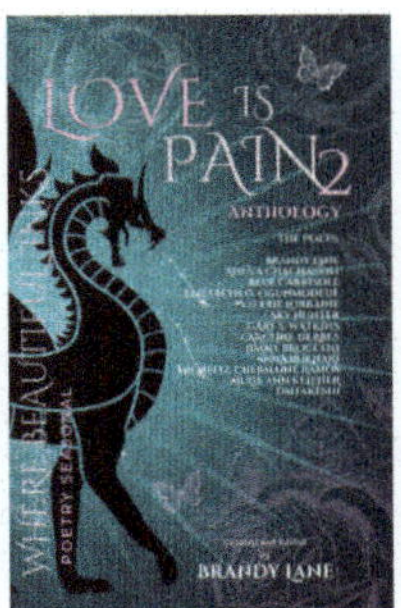

BRANDY LANE

NEW AUTHORS

COLLABORATIONS